Summer of the Wild Pig

Summer of the Wild Pig

By

Sandy Dengler

Library of Congress Cataloging in Publication Data

Dengler, Sandy.
Summer of the wild pig.

SUMMARY: Isobel, a javelina, brings both problems and pleasure to a hard-pressed, west Texas homesteading family in 1881.
[1. Peccaries—Fiction. 2. Pigs—Fiction.
3. Texas—Fiction. 4. Christian life—Fiction]
I. Title.
PZ7.D4146Su [Fic] 79-15609
ISBN 0-8024-8429-8

Printed in the United States of America

Contents

1

The Wild Pig

That was a shot! Daniel was certain. Probably a rifle shot, too. He scrambled up out of the wash and ran toward the crest of the hill. He did not stop to think that sticking your head up over a hill when someone is shooting might be dangerous.

Ever since his parents had homesteaded this strip of West Texas river bottom, life had been boring. Dull. All work. Maybe here was some of the excitement he had read about in the dime novels.

Daniel was halfway to the top of the hill, struggling through the brush, when he heard scurrying noises ahead. He stopped and listened. Something or someone was coming over the hill toward him. Maybe it was outlaws!

The tasajillo* rattled off to Daniel's left, and a javelina*, a wild pig, crashed past and clattered on down the hill. To Daniel's right, a second pig burst out of the brush and bucketed off down the wash. So that was it—javelinas and someone shooting at them. Did the hunter get any? Daniel hurried forward, hoping that those stories about javelinas attacking people were not really true.

Daniel reached the crest of the hill and saw a familiar red head bob beyond the sotol†. "Chet!" he called. "Hey, Chet!"

Daniel liked to think of Chet as his best friend, but he was not sure Chet felt that way. After all, Chet was sixteen and Daniel only twelve. Grown men do not always want to be bothered with somebody younger. Still . . .

Daniel was huffing by the time he reached Chet's side. Chet already had his skinning knife out and had just stuck the dead javelina.

"Here, Dan. Grab a hind leg."

Daniel did, and together the boys hoisted the javelina off the ground.

Chet grunted. "Gotta bleed 'er, or the meat won't be good. Pretty big, huh? Bet she dresses out to be a good forty pounds of meat."

Daniel was almost as happy as if he himself had bagged the pig. "Your mom gonna make

---

*Tah-sa-HEE-yo; a spiny, much-branched cholla cactus.
*Hah-vah-LEE-na; the wild pig, peccary, or musk hog.
†SOH-tol; a yucca-like plant with long, coarse leaves bunched on a heavy stalk.

pork pie out of him?"

"Prob'ly. But it's a her, not a him. And a mama at that."

"How do you know?" Daniel asked.

Chet dropped his side, and the other hind leg slipped out of Daniel's hands. The pig went *thunk*. Chet said, "Look. I'll show you. And from now on, you start observing. Remember what I said?"

"Yeah, I remember." Daniel was sorry he had forgotten. If Chet had told him once, he had told him a thousand times: if you want to learn anything, keep your eyes open.

Chet rolled the pig on its back and knelt beside it. He poked the pig here and there as he explained. "These are the milk bags. And see? You can squeeze a little milk out. That means she has a baby around here somewhere."

"Maybe it ran off with the others."

Chet nodded. "Prob'ly. They herd together—real family sorts."

Chet handed his rifle to Daniel and started dressing out his pig. Daniel watched fascinated as Chet slit the belly skin, flicking the knife about. Daniel braced himself—he did not like looking at animals' insides. But the way Chet did it, the whole unpleasant insides came out in one neat, membrane-wrapped package. You could not see the various parts at all. Chet could do anything well. Just anything.

Dry leaves rattled in the sotol. The boys jumped and turned toward the sound. Daniel thought of stories he had heard about how javelinas seek vengeance. And Chet had just killed one of them.

A tiny pig not even a foot high stumbled out of the sotol and started running. With a whoop the boys chased after it. Daniel yelped in pain as a lechuguilla* spine speared him in the shin. He kept running.

The baby pig ducked into a close clump of tasajillo. Chet's arm plunged in after it. Chet came out of the cactus with a thousand stickers in his arm, but he had the baby by one foot. The little pig squirmed free and ran for some rocks nearby.

Daniel dived for it. His elbow burned and his knees clunked as he skidded to a stop on the rocky ground. But he had a good tight hold on the baby pig's hindquarters. He lay on the hot stones until Chet could get an even better grip on the shrieking, writhing piglet.

The boys looked at each other. They giggled. They laughed. They could not quit laughing. Daniel's shirt was torn and his elbow scuffed. He had dirt and bruises on both knees. Chet's arm and hand were just full of cactus stickers.

Chet sat down with the piglet locked between his knees. He grinned. "A sorry sight we

---

*lay-chu-GEE-ya; a short, stiff agave with very hard, sharp spines on the leaf tips.

are! How can such a tiny little girl lead us such a merry chase!"

Daniel plopped down beside him and studied the pig more closely. "That's a girl, too, huh?"

"Yeah. What are you gonna name her?"

Daniel glanced up. "What do you mean, me? It's your pig."

Chet shrugged. "I killed the mama for meat, but you caught the baby. Besides, those lion hounds of ours would tear her apart. But your old Brown Bess wouldn't never hurt her. In fact, Bess might take over mothering her. She needs a mama."

Daniel thought a moment. "Yeah, Bess might. She took in an orphan lamb once. Chet, could I really have her?"

"Sure. We can't take her. If you bottle-raise her she might make a neat pet. I don't know. I never heard of anyone keeping a javelina before."

"Guess it's worth a try. Thanks, Chet. Thanks a lot!"

"Don't mention it."

Daniel curled the fingers of his right hand firmly around the piglet's knobby little legs and wrapped his left around her neck. She jerked and struggled, but he had her. Chet walked back to his downed pig and picked up his knife.

Daniel followed. "Chet, can I help you haul her home?"

"No, I can handle it. She's lighter without the insides. Mom might want the guts to make sausage casings, but I've no mind to carry all that back. Weather's too warm anyway, the insides will spoil fast. You take your orphan there home. I can carry this."

Daniel burbled his thanks again (sounding too much like a little kid, he thought later) and ran off toward home.

Two years ago, home would have been a shabby little farm in Illinois. Now it was an even shabbier farm in West Texas. Daniel remembered how Pop complained just before they had moved West. "Eighteen seventy-nine is going to be written off as the worst, the poorest, the meanest year in American history." Well, now it was 1881, and it did not seem a bit different from 1879. To Daniel, one year had seemed just like another—until now.

This year, if it appeared in history books, would be the year of Daniel's wild pig, his javelina. He loved her already. All head and knees, she was so ugly she was beautiful. Real pigs are nearly bald, but she had a coat of coarse, gray hair. The hair was much scratchier than the soft dog-fur on Brown Bess. She looked and felt like a pig and yet not a pig. She was exotic, remarkable, an animal Daniel's friends back in Illinois could never imagine, let alone believe.

Daniel was nearly in the ranch yard when he began to think about what Mom would say. Pop would not care. The girls would be delighted. But Mom was a practical woman, and there was nothing practical about bottle-raising a baby javelina.

Daniel went to the barn first. The squirming piglet had been a vexation all the way home. His hands were so tired of holding her they ached. He stepped into the cool shed and paused, waiting for his eyes to adjust from brilliant sun to dark shadows. He wandered around from end to end. What could he keep his baby pig in? Under the workbench in the corner stood a nail keg, and there were only a pound or two of nails left in the bottom. He dumped the keg out onto the bench top. He would put the nails in a box or something else later. This was perfect! Carefully he set the baby in the bottom of the keg and watched.

She was terrified. She had never, of course, been in such close quarters. Small as she was, she could barely turn around in there. On the other hand, she could not get out, either. And she surely tried. Satisfied that his little pig was safe, Daniel arranged some straw in the bottom and carried his precious nail keg to the house.

The kitchen smelled wonderful. Sometimes, when Mom was making soap or something like that, it smelled funny. But today stew beef bubbled on the stove, a big pot of it with onions, carrots, and potatoes. Daniel smelled biscuits in the oven, too.

Mom sat at the little table by the window sorting through beans. It was a job she hated, and she had learned to finish it fast. In one smooth motion she spilled and spread a scoop of beans. Then, with swift jerks she flicked out all the tiny stones and shriveled black no-goods. She would scrape those beans over the edge into a gunny sack and just as quickly have another scoop spread out. Daniel loved to watch.

Daniel's three sisters were setting the table for supper, teasing and jostling and arguing. As usual, nine-year-old Grace was telling seven-year-old Rachel exactly what to do. And as usual, Rachel was doing it her own way. Baby Naomi's only job was to put out the plates, one at a time.

"Hi, Mom. I'm home," said Daniel helpfully.

Mom smiled. "About time. Supper's in ten minutes. Bring in a couple loads of wood first and wash your hands. And leave the nails outside."

Daniel licked his lips. "Uh, it's not nails. Not exactly."

Mom's hands stopped flicking across the beans. She sat upright. "Oh? Just what is it, exactly?"

Daniel tilted the keg. "Here. Look."

"What in creation . . . a wild pig! Daniel, I don't know how you came up with that bit of truck, but you'll dispose of it immediately. And look at your shirt! The sleeve there . . ."

Daniel did not hear the last half clearly (although he knew without hearing what she had said) because his sisters were suddenly swarming all around them, squealing and crying, "Let me see!" They oohed and aahed and admired.

Daniel usually did not go out of his way for his sisters, but this was an advantage. They often got what they asked for from Mom before he did. He encouraged their oohs and aahs by carefully tilting the keg toward Grace, then toward Rachel. He lowered it carefully so three-year-old Naomi could see.

He heard the door slam behind him. A fuzzy moustache tickled his cheek, and Pop was peering over his shoulder.

"Now where'd you ever get that, Dan?"

"Chet was out hunting behind our ten-acre bean patch. He killed the mother, and we caught this one. She's a girl."

Mom sighed. "Chet. I should have guessed."

Pop nodded. "Good. Let Chet shoot all the pigs he can. We can do without them ruining the beans. They root the seeds out before they get a chance to sprout. What are you gonna name her, Dan?"

Mom exploded. "Absolutely not! I can't think of a thing more useless than a wild pig! We have only the goat. Until we get a cow we don't have enough milk for the girls, let alone this pig."

Mom frequently mentioned the lack of a cow.

"Now, wait a minute, Martha. The boy can't just turn it loose."

"Then he can club it or drown it or . . ."

"Mom! I can't do that. 'Sides, it's one of God's creatures."

Pop continued. "You said yourself you wished we had a pig because you throw away a lot of scraps a hog could be turning into bacon. Parings, meat scraps, bean hulls. Well, here's your pig, just like you asked for."

"Raise her for a domestic hog? Hmpph! Then I'd have to listen to all the wails and moaning when butchering time came. And she's crafty. She'll escape in no time flat. There's no telling the damage she'd do. No. It can't be done."

But Mom was weakening. Daniel could see that. The girls knew better than to whine, but they were very good at begging for something without actually begging. And Mom always bowed to Pop's will eventually.

A few minutes later, when the family sat down to supper, the matter was settled in everyone's mind but Mom's. At least for the moment the little javelina had a home.

2

To Name a Pig

Church was especially stuffy today, it seemed. Daniel felt sticky and squirmy. Naomi was napping, draped against his arm. Pop was dozing a little (listened best with his eyes shut, he claimed). Mom, with Rachel and Grace on either side of her, shifted her attention between Pastor Dougald and the fidgety girls. It was a usual sort of Sunday service.

Daniel heard the Carson family in the pew behind, being every bit as fidgety. Whereas Daniel's family had three girls and a boy, the Carsons had just the opposite—a girl, Carrie (who was exactly Daniel's age), and three boys. The two little boys were all right, but Daniel was not very enthusiastic about the oldest, fourteen-year-old Matthew. Mom was always saying, "Why can't you be more like Matt?" "Matt gets his chores done without grumbling." "Matt acts grown up." Things like that. From where Daniel sat now, it sounded like

Matt was being just as fidgety as any less noble person.

Now Daniel's favorite part was coming. It was not because this was the final portion of the service. It was the way the pastor prayed aloud as the congregation was singing. Somehow the combined voices lifted both prayer and song higher than either could ascend alone. It made Daniel feel very good inside.

The congregation stood as someone across the room announced the hymn number. Then Carrie's clear soprano picked up the melody, and Daniel tried singing harmony to it. So many voices were singing he could do that without his errors being heard.

As the second verse commenced, Pastor Dougald spoke: "Lord, we call on You in adversity—" (a pause). "We praise You when the good things happen—" (another pause). "Now we ask that You help us learn to love You in all the other circumstances as well. Don't let us forget You for a moment. Let us think of You first when we rise in the morning. Let us fall asleep with Your name on our lips. Help us keep You in our hearts and in our minds as we make our daily walk. In Christ's precious name we give thanks and ask for Your guidance—" (a final pause). "Amen and amen!"

Daniel's voice strayed back to the melody line. He was singing without thinking now. His thoughts were on the pastor's prayer. How do you think about God all the time? Daniel was fairly certain that his mother was correct in her assumption that God exists. God was probably also big enough to keep an eye on every person all the time. But how can you see God? And how do you know for certain He is there, instead of just guessing or hoping so?

Keeping your mind on God was a pretty tall order when so many other things clamored for attention. And that reminded Daniel of his javelina. He had had her for over a week now. Protesting about the use of good milk, his mom had shown him how to give the little piglet milk and pap. Already the baby was nibbling radish greens and lettuce leaves. And she was starting to respond to his voice.

The hymn had ended, and the pastor was intoning the final blessing. There it was again—"The Lord make His countenance to shine upon you . . ." Countenance meant face. Said another way, May the Lord smile upon you all the time. A nice thought, but how do you smile back when you cannot even see the Lord's countenance?

Daniel tucked the puzzlement away in the back of his mind. He turned around to Carrie as soon as he could legally do so.

"Carrie! Come out to our wagon. I want to show you something!"

"Show me what?" Carrie followed eagerly.

They were outside before the pastor reached the door to commence handshaking. It was cool and breezy out, a delicious day.

Daniel jogged back to the lot where the horses and rigs were parked. Carrie followed right behind, jacking up her skirts a little so she could run better. They squeezed between the Murphy rig and the banker's phaeton, carefully past Mrs. Boye's horse (who bit), and clambered up into Pop's dirty gray farm wagon. Daniel pulled the nail keg out from under the seat.

"Look here, Carrie."

"Oh, Dan! Isn't it sweet! Is it a girl or a boy?"

"A girl. She's real tame now. Here. You hold her." Dan lifted her out into Carrie's arms, waiting lest the pig squirm free. But the baby seemed to know when it was appreciated. It nestled snugly into Carrie's muslin dress.

"What's her name, Dan?"

"I don't know. I can't think of one. Madderafact, I was hoping you could help me pick one."

Carrie pondered the problem. She touched her fingers to the baby's mouth, and the pig slurped them. "You charming little thing! Look at her nose go! She's so ugly she's beautiful. How about Clarabelle? I have a doll named Clarabelle. It means bright and beautiful. Or Isobel? Isobel means something beautiful that's devoted to God."

" 'Devoted to God.' Like what Pastor Dougald was saying this morning. Talking about everything being for God."

Carrie nodded. "Even your little javelina here."

Daniel smiled. "I knew you'd think of the perfect name. You're an expert on names. Isobel. I like that very much. Thanks, Carrie."

And Carrie smiled back.

Over the next few days Isobel, with her grand new name, seemed to grow even faster. Soon she came whenever Daniel called her. True, bribery was involved. Daniel fed her some snack each time she came. Mom insisted she be weaned early, to save the milk, but Isobel thrived anyway.

Isobel's head was so big and her neck so bulky that a collar slipped right off. So Daniel and his father fashioned a sort of harness from rope. Now Daniel could take Isobel for walks out into the desert. It was an unpleasant thought, but someday he might have to turn her loose. So he wanted her to know what her natural home was like.

Brown Bess usually came along on these outings. She was an old dog now. She moved slowly and barked less often. Her long, shaggy coat was faded and ratty looking. "Full of years," the Bible's way of saying it, was most appropriate. White hairs flecked her muzzle, and her back swayed. And as Chet had suggested, she had become mother to Isobel.

At first Bess would have nothing to do with

the piglet. Bess hated javelinas, as well as coyotes, ground squirrels, and jays. But after Isobel spent her first two nights crying, Bess's mother instinct had taken over. Now the two were inseparable companions. They were together so much, in fact, that Daniel no longer penned Isobel up. He knew she would be wherever Bess was. And the old dog, getting fatter by the day, stayed close to the house.

The moon waxed and waned, and suddenly the month of May was getting old. One day—one month, for that matter—looked much like another to Daniel. The daily chores never ended, and each thing came in its season. But his parents were starting to worry about winter already, and here was summer just starting. They talked about the drought and the poor crops. But, thought Daniel, West Texas is always dry—drier than Illinois by a long shot.

Sometimes his folks included Daniel in their conversations. For instance, one evening during supper, Pop asked him, "Say, Dan. You've been out wandering a lot with that pig. Seen any cattle around?"

"Cattle. Nope. What kind of cattle?"

"Big, apparently. Carson came across some cloven tracks around that tinaja* between his place and ours. Biggest cow tracks he ever saw, he says."

Daniel waved his fork. "You know, Pop, now

---

*Tee-NAH-hah; a natural water hole or pothole.

you mention it—Chet says he saw some mighty big tracks in Tornado Wash, and he opined it might be one of Wesmorton's bulls."

He stopped. There, it had happened again. Every time he mentioned Chet or Chet's family the air turned cold. His parents continued eating in chilly silence. He quit talking and resumed eating, too. No need to tell them Chet thought it might be a bull with three or four cows.

Pop shook his head. "Ain't Wesmorton's. Carson thought so, too, but all Wes's stock is accounted for."

Silence again.

Pop must have felt the chill, too. He brightened up his voice and changed the subject. "Have you taken notice of Bess lately?"

"What about her?"

"I think she's in a family way."

Grace always talked with her mouth full. "What does that mean?"

"It means," said Daniel, "that she's gonna have puppies. Are you sure, Pop?"

Pop shrugged. "Not real sure. She's so fat you can't really tell. But she's sure acting like it."

"Wouldn't that be great! Bess won't be around too much longer, but her puppies would. I'd sure love to have a couple of her children."

"*One* of her children," Mom corrected.

"One then. Maybe we could give the Carsons one, too. Carrie would like that. She admires Brown Bess."

"You bet we'll give the Carsons one," Pop chuckled. "Whose dog do you think the daddy is?"

"Ira!" Mom hushed. "Little pitchers have big ears."

"What does that mean?" asked Rachel.

Grace snapped, "It means, Rachel, that you'll hear something you shouldn't know about. Except, I already know all about that stuff." She smiled boastfully, then glanced about at the cold stares. The smile faded quickly, and she tackled her mashed potatoes with sudden vigor.

3

The Wild Bull

The biggest difference between Illinois and West Texas, decided Daniel, was the seasons. Illinois had crisp winter, soggy spring, muggy summer with lightning bugs, and a week or two of glorious autumn color. But Illinois also had between-seasons: before winter but after autumn, when the iron-gray sky drizzled shadows out of existence; and non-spring, before and after it was truly spring, with lots more cloudy days, rain, and dampness. It sometimes even turned cold and drizzly in midsummer.

But not so Texas! When spring arrived it was there. Summer came early, but stayed like it ought—hot and dry and sunny with a rare thunderstorm. There were few trees to turn color except for the sycamores down by the river. The willows tried, but never having had maples as examples, they just did not measure up. And winter, although cooler, was usually as sunny as any other season. Daniel, who had always disliked digging his way to the barn through snow, loved Texas winters.

Now the last of May, spring was gone and summer was upon them. There had been no rain for weeks, so the temporary waterholes here and there were starting to dry up. The cactus—except for the barrels—were done blooming. The dainty annuals were long since gone.

Daniel basked in the warm morning sun and wiggled his toes in the cool sand of Whipsnake Wash. His shoes hung around his neck, the laces knotted behind, just in case he got into stickers or lechuguilla. But he was able to go barefoot off and on all year in this country. Marvelous!

Out on the end of twenty feet of clothesline rope, Isobel scruffed and snorted and dug about. She had fought the leash at first. But now she was either accustomed to it or resigned to it. She was even figuring out how to unwrap herself when she ended up on the wrong side of a bush from her master. Smart pig!

A pert sparrow with a black throat posed atop a cholla* and tuned up for a concert. Suddenly it cheeped a warning and dived into the low brush. Isobel thrust her piggy snout in

---

*CHOY-uh; branching cactus shaped somewhat like a little tree. The joints are cylindrical.

the air and snorted. What was out there? Daniel stood up, not stopping to think that he might startle something dangerous.

A dark brown longhorn cow came lumbering around the bend of the wash not ten rods away. She was headed right his way. Daniel stood still, but she saw him anyway. She stopped stifflegged and blasted air out her nostrils. Daniel heard other hoofed feet behind her, crackling in the brush and stones. The brown cow bolted and quickly disappeared the way she had come.

Longhorns! Where did they come from? No one in the immediate area raised longhorns. And there were the stories Daniel remembered. The stories told how longhorns, a curious breed, would approach a man on foot, first from curiosity, next from a growing anger, and then would trample that horseless, luckless person to death. Surely the stories were not true. These cattle had turned and run. But . . .

The brush rattled nearby. There was no place to hide. Daniel hunched down beside the rocks, hoping his shirt, made grey by countless launderings, would look like just another rock.

Across the wash a bull stepped out of the brush. He was the hugest bull Daniel had ever seen. The massive beast took two steps forward and paused. He was sniffing the air in huge breaths, looking for something. For Daniel? He shook his head, and six feet of longhorns swayed up and down. The bull was white. All white. It was not like any bull back East. Daniel had been frightened enough by the Jerseys and Ayrshires in Illinois. But they were nothing compared with this menacing presence. All neck and shoulders, he loomed against the sky like a monstrous, bovine mountain. He snorted, pawed, and took another step.

Suddenly Isobel squealed and ran past Daniel. She lunged to the end of her leash and stopped hard, almost falling. If he was afraid before, Daniel was petrified now. Isobel was not only putting herself in danger—she might betray him as well.

But the bull apparently considered javelinas beneath his dignity. He looked around once more, wheeled, and disappeared without a sound into the underbrush. How could such a massive, forbidding animal make no noise at all?

Daniel was afraid to move. Had the longhorns moved on or was that gargantuan bull waiting out there silently, ready to charge as soon as he moved? Daniel sat until his frazzled nerves allowed him to sit no longer. He stepped cautiously out into the wash. There was no sound. A sparrow with a black throat—the same or another—started singing nearby. Reassured, Daniel gathered in most of Isobel's leash and started running, dragging her along. It had taken them nearly an hour to meander over to Whipsnake Wash. Daniel made it back to the farm, safe at last, in eleven minutes flat.

"Look at the size of that gunner's feet! Dan'l, how tall did you say he was?" Mr. Carson was squatting down, tracing with his finger the bull's track in the sand of Whipsnake Wash.

"I don't know. I'm not much good at estimating stuff like that. But when he shook his head and his horns waved up and down they didn't come near touching that tasajillo there."

Pop wagged his head. "Six feet at the shoulder if he's an inch! Sure like to see that piece of beef."

Mr. Carson stood up. "Bet he'd dress out to a thousand pounds. Glad you brought us here, Dan'l. At least now we know for sure what the bruiser looks like."

Then Mr. Carson, Matt, Pop, and Daniel stood around for lack of anything better to do. The bull was no longer about. In fact, it was yesterday that Daniel had come running home with his story. And now he felt proud. Not only had Pop and Mr. Carson believed him, but they had taken the trouble to come way out here.

Matt wandered off down the wash a bit. "Here's that brown cow's track, Pa. Where she saw Daniel and turned and ran."

The group reconvened at the new location. "Your average size cow," mumbled Pop. "Little on the large size maybe. Whaddaya think, Carson?"

Mr. Carson turned to Daniel. "You sure the bull was white? No brown brindle on his neck?"

Daniel shrugged. "I didn't see any brown. But I saw him mostly from straight on. And—uh—I was a little scared."

Mr. Carson grunted. "I bet. I woulda been scared witless. Only bull that comes close to being white is Wesmorton's, and it has enough brown on it to be noticed. Looks like we have wild longhorns, maybe crossed the river from Mexico. Don't think they were raised here, or we woulda seen some sign before now."

The group ambled back toward Daniel's house.

Pop nodded. "Matt, you best not go rabbit hunting anymore until we know more about this animal. Or else take along the buffalo gun instead of your .20-gauge."

Matt laughed "Mr. Tremain, a buffalo gun would disintegrate the rabbit. Mom would have a hard time making rabbit pie out of two feet and a fluff-tail."

The men laughed, but Daniel did not. He did not know what "disintegrate" meant, and besides, he did not have much time for listening to Matt. Matt was always acting so grown-up.

Daniel fell in beside his father, trying to match stride for stride and not quite managing. "Pop, are they really dangerous?"

"I never met any personally. But I heard enough stories to say yeah, I suspect they might be."

"Funny," Daniel said, "back in Illinois you can't trust a bull. Even the milk-herd bulls will turn on you. So you just stay out of the bull pasture. But this one, Pop, this one was looking for me. Looking for trouble. The bulls back home don't go hunting for you."

Pop nodded. "Dan, this is home now. Illinois is past. And don't forget that right now you're walking through a bull pasture a county big."

Daniel shuddered. "Mom's been talking so much about getting a cow. Hope one doesn't come walking into our yard to get her."

Mr. Carson laughed. "No fear. These cattle won't come near a human habitation."

"A what?"

"Buildings. Where people are. They're wild as coyotes. They stay away from settlements."

Daniel thought to himself that he had seen coyotes within ten feet of his bedroom window. But he said nothing. For one thing he was still trying to match strides with his father and still having no success. When they reached the Tremain homestead he had not yet found the rhythm.

That Sunday after church the Carsons invited the Tremains to dinner. It was hot—hotter than usual—so the mothers decided to make a picnic of Sunday dinner and eat down in the wash behind the house. Good! Daniel liked picnics. For one thing, no one yelled at you for putting your elbows on the table because there was no table. You could use your fingers as long as you did not slurp. And you could reach for seconds without drawing attention to yourself by having to ask, "Pass the whatever."

As the two wagons rattled onto the Carson homestead, Daniel thought about the trim white houses and red barns of Illinois and how different the Carson farm was. The buildings looked ready to collapse, although they were sturdy and made of adobe. In Illinois a flat roof would cave in under snow the first winter, but here it did not matter.

The whole compound was fenced in with wobbly, crooked mesquite rails. The gate was wired together. And yet everything was clean and orderly—the house to the right, the sty (although the Carsons did not have pigs yet) off to the far right, the corrals and milk shed to the left. There seemed acres of room in the vast, open ranch yard.

The men parked the wagons under the tree by the house. As Daniel hopped down he sensed something missing. What was it?

Of course! That was it! Daniel paused on the porch. "Carrie! Where's Brunhilde and Zack? There's no welcoming committee here to knock us over."

Carrie laughed and plopped down on the porch swing. "We rented them out."

"You rented out two dogs? Who would pay to use two dogs?"

"Ramon Guirran. He couldn't find enough hands for spring round-up. He heard how good our two dogs are at herding cattle, so he came over and borrowed them. For a nice bit of money, too."

"He's not getting a bad deal."

"Especially not with Brunny. When it comes to herding cows she's as good as any man on horseback."

Silence. The little kids were off somewhere. The parents were inside. What do you do? Carrie swung back and forth. Matt leaned against the porch post. They were too big for kids' games, but not interested in much else. Matt said something, but Daniel did not hear it.

Matt repeated, "I said, Dan, do you remember that white bull?"

"I haven't forgotten that fellow yet."

"Well, we're finding his tracks in the washes right close by. Right near the yard here."

"Because the dogs are gone, I bet. No one to chase him off."

"That's what we were thinking."

More silence.

Carrie pulled out a length of yarn and knotted the ends. Swiftly she slipped the loop over her hands. "Learned a new cat's cradle from Melody Hawes this morning. Watch—if I can remember it."

She flicked her fingers in and out, flubbed it, and started over. In triumph she squealed, "This is it!" It looked like a royal tangle to Daniel, but she pulled her little fingers free, and the pattern fell into place between her out-stretched hands, an intricate lacework of triangles and zigzags. "It's called Apache Door. Melanie says she learned it from an Indian, but I don't believe her. You know Melanie."

Daniel grinned. "I sure do! She was telling me how her uncle was a hero in the Civil War. I found out from her cousin he was a regimental blacksmith and always two days behind in his work."

Carrie shook her fingers loose. "Wonder why people boast like that?"

Daniel wondered, too. But he wondered more why some people never did. Here was Matt, accomplished in so many ways and considered a man at fourteen. And he never boasted. Then Matt was asking Carrie to show him the cat's cradle. He really seemed hungry to learn new things—any things.

But Carrie never finished the lesson. The fathers came around the corner from the springhouse, the mothers appeared with the picnic hampers, and they all left the yard. Matt and Grace helped carry the hampers, and Naomi whined the whole way.

Naomi was not the only cranky one. It had taken Daniel a long time to wangle permission to bring Isobel along. And now she was acting terrible. She yanked and squealed and fought the leash. She tried to bite Rachel. Daniel was having second thoughts about keeping a javelina as a pet, but he certainly was not about to admit it. Isobel would grow up and grow out of her babyish ways any month now. Daniel would endure and discipline and look forward to the day when she was a mature pig who behaved properly.

Grace and Rachel reached the wash first, so they got to choose the picnic spot. The mothers had the cloths laid out by the time Daniel arrived, his pig lurching from one side to the other. Daniel did not feel inclined to lead, but he surely did not like being last like this, either.

The menu was quail with trimmings. Mr. Carson boasted extensively about Matt's hunting prowess. To shoot enough cottontops to feed two families was quite an accomplishment. Daniel thought so, too, but Matt did not seem much impressed with his own good hunting. In fact, when Mr. Carson called him a regular Nimrod, Matt turned red and said, "Please, Pa, not Nimrod." But Daniel never did learn why Matt objected to the allusion.

Dinner conversation shifted from drought to the mysterious white bull to cows in general.

Mrs. Carson said, "Our Rosita isn't giving milk like she used to. We're going to have to bring off another calf soon. Ira, do you have any suggestions about finding a good milking bull?"

Daniel's pop rubbed his chin thoughtfully. "No, Clara, I've never come across a bull you can milk."

"Ira, you scalawag!" Mrs. Carson exploded.

"You know what I mean. A bull to—I mean—" She glanced about at the giggling children. "I'll talk to you later."

Pop grinned. "Don't talk to me. Talk to Will Peterson. He has a fine milk herd. I almost bought a heifer from him last fall, but his prices were too high for my pockets to reach."

Mom's head snapped around, and she stared at him. Obviously she had not known that.

As to Rosita, Daniel thought he heard her up at the Carson house. Her distant moo was unsettling somehow. Daniel felt silly thinking that way. What could be ominous about an old milk cow's moo?

The children started back to the house before the adults did. Daniel was again at the tag end of the parade, tugging at his truculent pig. He even tied her leash to his wrist so that she could not jerk it out of his hands.

"Oh, oh!" said Matt as they entered the yard. "Someone left the gate open." He swung it shut, and Daniel helped slip the wire loop over the gatepost.

The blue-and-white setting hen strutted disdainfully out across the ranch yard. With a squeal Naomi took off, running after it and waving her arms. If she had been told once about chasing chickens, she had been told . . .

Daniel started after her. This time she was going to get paddled! Over by the milk shed Rosita mooed again.

"Naomi Tremain, you cut that ou—" Daniel

froze in terror. Rosita was not alone. Beside the milk shed stood the huge white bull.

Naomi stopped. Even at three, she knew mortal danger when it was standing right in front of her. The bull rumbled and shook his head toward her. The mile-wide horns wagged.

Over by the house someone screamed—Carrie?—and Grace's voice said something about fetching Pop.

The bull lowered his head, his nose nearly touching the dirt. Beside Daniel, Matt cried, "Oh, God, help me!" Then Matt was gone, running toward the house. Daniel could not believe it. Matt was leaving him alone out here. *That coward! That yellow . . .*

Daniel cried out, "Naomi! Drop down! Lie flat on your tummy, hear me?"

But Naomi did not. Crying, she turned and ran right to Daniel. The bull snorted and lurched forward.

Daniel did not think. He ran at his tiny sister. He wrapped himself around her and threw her down, sprawling on top of her. He tried to pin her kicking legs under his own so they could not move.

At the same moment Isobel, squealing, hit the end of her leash and started running in a wide arc around them. Out of the corner of his eye Daniel saw Isobel run between the bull and himself. The bull swung his massive head up and veered away. The pig had distracted and confused him. He jogged over to the pigsty and wheeled. Dust boiled up around his dinner-plate feet.

Had anyone thought to open the gate? Probably not. The bull was trapped, penned into a human habitation. He bellowed and dropped his head again. Naomi squirmed and almost got to her knees. Daniel wrestled her down and pinned her again, but the bull had chosen his target.

Daniel could hear him coming, making the whole ground vibrate. Then Isobel's staccato feet were running too. She nearly pulled his arm out of joint when she hit the end of her leash this time. Confined to twenty feet of clothesline, she was surely as terrified as Daniel.

The bull veered off again, his nose high. He paced over to the milk shed. The dewlap under his throat and the heavy skin beneath his belly flopped and swayed. Rosita lowed, and he answered—a high bugling call.

Daniel struggled with Naomi. He must not accidentally let her up again. Suddenly, somehow, Daniel sensed a change in the bull. The canny longhorn was calculating the way out. And he had identified his enemy. That wiggly pile in the middle of the yard—the one with a Sunday shirttail flapping—was the enemy. The javelina was not. Daniel could see and feel the difference in the bull's mind. The monster would not be distracted again.

Daniel would just have to run for it. The

corncrib was closest. He would go for that and hope someone had opened the gate. Gripping Naomi tightly, Daniel bolted to his feet.

But Naomi's skirt—Daniel was standing on it! And it would not rip loose! Now the bull's head was down again. Now he was lunging forward, big as a freight train. There was no escape now. They were lost.

From nowhere, Matt was by Daniel's side. He dropped to one knee, steady as a rock. The long blue barrel of the buffalo gun was by his cheek. The air exploded by Daniel's ear.

The bull hesitated. Its knees buckled. With a hoarse bellow it dropped. The tip of the nearest longhorn scuffed into the dirt nearly close enough for Daniel to touch it.

Silence. After the gunshot, the bellow, the thunderous *whump!*—silence.

Sobbing, dusty little Naomi wrapped herself tightly around Daniel. Then Mom was there to scoop her up. Matt laid the Sharps down quietly and buried his face in his trembling hands.

Heady confusion was swirling all around as women wept and men roared, but Daniel did not hear it. He could only stare at the bull. He had called Matt a coward. What a stupid mistake! Thank goodness he had not said it aloud. At least he did not think he had. What surprised him most was the change Matt's presence had made. His fear had left. Even with that bull charging down on them, when Matt was beside him he had not felt lost or frightened at all.

Now his attention was grabbed by Mr. Carson's strident roar. "Who left that gate open?"

Pop looked around. "Who went out last when we left the yard?"

Mr. Carson was red-faced with rage. "I told you people a million times to *keep that gate shut!*"

"For pity sakes!" screamed Mrs. Carson. "It's all over! You can talk civil to your friends and family now. Just keep your voice down, will you?"

Mr. Carson's face was as dark and twisted as an Illinois tornado. "Dan'l? You?"

Daniel cringed. "I don't remember. Maybe. Isobel was giving me a hard time, and I was concentrating on keeping her in line. Maybe I was. I don't remember, sir."

Mom wailed. "That pig! That pig is a disaster!"

"Now wait a minute, Martha," Pop cut in. "If it weren't for that pig dashing around and distracting the bull, half your children would be dead now." (Daniel caught his breath. He had not thought of that). Pop's voice continued, firm and quiet. "So the bull got in. I bet he wanted to add Rosita to his harem but couldn't get to her except through the yard. But it's Daniel who saved Naomi, and it's that pig saved both of them—gave Matt time to fetch the Sharps."

Mr. Carson took a deep breath and tugged his waistcoat down smooth. "Yeah. Gave Matt time to fetch the Sharps. He knew the very square inch to hit, too. Did you see, Ira? Right between the eyes. Right in the middle of the curl. You know, Ira, it's the only place—the *only* place—that'll stop a charging bull cold. I'm mighty proud of you, Matt."

Matt shook his head. "Weren't me, Pa. I didn't know—almost couldn't decide whether to aim for his heart or his head. It's as if I weren't the one doing the aiming. Pa, don't you see God's hand in this?"

Mom licked her lips, almost embarrassed. "I—uh—I see the hands of two very brave boys, for sure. And they're shaking as bad as mine are. Let's all go in and have some tea and try to calm down."

Just the thing! Everyone agreed. Pop and Mr. Carson started talking about butchering—the meat would spoil quickly in the hot weather, so they would have to spread it around to the neighbors quickly. And jerk plenty for dog food.

Without thinking, Daniel drew the clothesline in until Isobel was close to his side. Isobel. A lovely thing devoted to God. Was Matt right—that God had ordained the little pig to be in just the right place at just the right time? Or perhaps the whole thing would never have happened at all, if only Isobel had not been there. Then Daniel would have remembered to close the gate. Or would he . . . Daniel was more confused than ever.

"Daniel? Coming?" Carrie was calling from the porch.

"Coming!" Daniel replied. One thing sure—Matt had asked God for help and now was convinced he had received it. Daniel thought again how safe and relieved he had felt when Matt was there beside him. Matt, of all people. It was as if Daniel had this moment met Matt for the first time. Daniel would not ignore him again.

4

Brown Bess's Pups

Bess disappeared the morning of the first day in June. Isobel was distraught. Lost and dejected, she did nothing but follow at Daniel's heels out to the woodshed and back, out to the barn and back, out to the springhouse and back. Daniel understood her consternation. He was worried, too.

Isobel, of course, had no idea what was happening, but Daniel knew why Bess had gone into hiding. She wanted to be alone when she brought her litter into the world. She had always been that way. But what if something happened to her while she was giving birth? She was an old dog to be bearing puppies. And she was vulnerable to any coyote or bobcat that might happen by.

Early next morning, however, Brown Bess was back on the stoop outside the kitchen door, as always, waiting for her breakfast. The girls all greeted her as though she had been gone a year. Mom gave her some goat milk with her scraps. Pop checked her over carefully and pronounced her a healthy mother. But although everyone searched, no one could find where she had hidden her pups.

Actually, Daniel and Pop were too busy to search diligently. The woodshed was nearly empty, and Daniel had found a dead tree down along the river. It took them three days to cut it into cordwood and another day to haul the wood in. Daniel had blisters on his hands as they stacked the last of the dead tree into the woodshed. He was proud of his blisters. He was doing a man's work.

As he lay in bed that night he wondered if God were proud, too. He had not thought about God for days. Did He care? God was watching over Bess's puppies, wherever they were. Mom had said so. Carrie had said that, too. She believed in God just as unshakeably as Mom did. Matthew believed, obviously, so faith was not entirely a woman's providence. But Chet did not.

Here was another confusing thing. His parents were always bad-mouthing Chet's family. Unchurched, Mom called them. And unwashed. Unprincipled, Pop said. Can not trust them. Daniel did not mention these opinions to Chet, of course. He was afraid Chet might think some of it was rubbing off on him. They just did not understand Chet, that was all.

Of course, it made Daniel uncomfortable

when Chet laughed at God and ridiculed church-going. But then, who was to say Chet was wrong and everyone else was right? No one had ever seen God, to prove the matter one way or the other. Ah, well. The answers would come with time. For days Daniel had been too busy to take Isobel for a walk. Tomorrow morning he would do that.

He fell asleep thinking not about God, or even about Chet, but about Isobel.

The next morning Daniel had a lot of trouble getting started. His intention to take Isobel out was frustrated by one thing after another. Mom needed wood brought in. Pop could not find the rake attachment for the cultivator. Then the chickens got out, and Mom needed Daniel as well as the girls to chase them back into their pen. Rachel tore her shoe during the chicken-herding venture, and Daniel had to sew it for her. Her fingers were not strong enough to force the needle through the leather.

It was halfway to noon when he finally tied the harness and leash to Isobel. Bess appeared out of nowhere, running with the heavy, lumbering waddle she had developed lately.

"Come along, Bess! The exercise will do you good!"

Together the three friends crossed the springwash behind the house and angled up the ridge toward Porksaddle.

The sky was overcast, the air hot and muggy. Daniel's face was sweaty before they reached the ridgetop. Pop said a good sign of rain was when the swallows flew down low. As Daniel came out on the ridgetop a white-throated swift swished past his ear. *Do swifts count for rain omens?* he wondered.

Beyond Gopher Canyon, Porksaddle Mountain did not look much like a mountain at all. It was just another blocky little desert peak, sparcely clad in scrub. A dull gray haze in the canyon made the peak look even smaller than it was. Now the air was starting to smell even more like rain coming.

Daniel was carefully practicing Chet's admonition to be observant. He noticed a mound of cholla joints that was a pack rat nest. He noticed also that all the joints were old and dried up. Something had caught the pack rat, and this nest was abandoned. There was a wren nest in a tasajillo thicket. A double row of dots in the dust marked the passage of a pinacate beetle the night before. Daniel was feeling rather proud of himself.

Now they were in the midst of an area where javelinas had been, and recently too. Daniel saw where the wild pigs had torn up the prickly pear cactus. Broken pads lay all over—a blessing to the cactus, since some of those pads would take root and start new cactus patches. The pigs were obviously after the tunas, the prickly pear fruits, although they were still a little green.

Daniel traced the little cloven pig-tracks in

the loose dirt. He noticed marks where the pigs had been rooting about searching for grubs. The sign was fresh. Very fresh.

Bess pressed in close to his legs, uneasy. She did not like javelinas—Isobel being a notable exception, of course—and her hair bristled on her back. The pigs must indeed be close. Daniel kept a tight grip on Isobel's leash. What if she decided to take off and join her wild cousins?

The sky scowled darker. Daniel felt more and more uneasy. With a word to Bess he turned and started toward home, back down the ridge. The day felt very thick and heavy.

Bess stopped so suddenly Daniel almost tripped over her. She growled. Isobel grunted, curious. A javelina stood on the trail facing them, not twenty feet ahead. It was bigger than the one Chet had shot last spring. It snuffled. It raised its pointy snout and clicked its teeth together.

Daniel heard a slight noise off to one side. It was another pig. There were pigs all over. They were ominously silent, waving their snouts in the sullen air.

Should he holler and flap his arms or would that be worse than just standing still? Daniel did not know. The sweat on his face was not from the heat now. His palms were wet, too.

The pig ahead took a jerky little step forward and grunted again. Isobel squealed and tugged on her leash. Daniel yanked the leash back without thinking, intending to scoop Isobel up in his arms. She squealed louder in protest, a shrill piggy scream.

Daniel could not tell exactly what happened next. The pig in front of them took a step forward. Bess lunged at it with a snarl. Dog and pig met, tangling in a swirl of dust. Then another pig was joining the melee. Daniel started grabbing rocks and hurling them, shouting. Bess yelped. The pigs were snorting and running away in all directions through the brush, clattering. There must have been a dozen of them.

Daniel was still holding onto Isobel's leash, and she was still tugging this way and that, all excited. He stopped throwing rocks. There was nothing left to throw them at.

Bess was lying on the ridge trail where the pig had stood. Bess, who had traveled with them to West Texas all the way from Union County, Illinois. Bess, who was older even than Daniel. Bess, defending her best friend, Isobel, and her master, Daniel. Bess, who had lived such a warm, friend-filled life, full of years. Bess, a brand new mother.

Bess was dead.

It had started raining around noon, and it was still raining as they finished their supper. Only Rachel and Naomi had left the table. It was their bedtime. Mom and Pop were very quiet. Grace was still snuffling a little. She had cried the most.

"Well," Mom said finally, "now we *do* have to find those puppies."

"They can't be too far off," Pop mused. "Bess hung around the yard most of the time. Bet they're within a hundred yards of us right now."

"We will save the puppies, won't we?" Grace sniffled.

"We'll do our best." But Mom did not sound very confident.

"Pop, why did they attack us? Javelinas are supposed to be scared of dogs and people."

"Well now, Dan. Did they attack, or did Bess? And you said Isobel was squealing. She was one of their own. I can't say whether they had in mind to rescue her, but I bet they were plenty curious. Besides, they knew that in a fair fight an old, weak dog like Bess is no match for a wild pig."

"Bess wasn't weak!" snapped Grace.

"She was, too," Daniel argued. "She hadn't gotten her strength back yet from having those puppies. And she's old. Older'n me, even. I mean, she *was* old. Fourteen. That's old for a dog."

"Since you know so much about dogs, Mr. Know-All, where did she put her puppies?"

"If I knew, do you think I'd be sitting here?"

Mom broke in. "That's enough, both of you! Dan, you needn't shout. We understand you're upset. We all are. But you just keep a closer rein on yourself. Grace, red the table up, and start the dishes." The way Mom said it left no room for argument. Pouting, Grace halfheartedly commenced stacking the dirty dinner plates.

Pop said, "I don't imagine how we're gonna find puppies in this dark in the rain, but we'd better check all the obvious places tonight."

"But Pop, we already looked everywhere, right when she first had them."

"She might have moved them in closer. In fact, she probably did. I'll take the haymow and barn. Dan, you search the woodshed. You've seen her come and go. Where did she come and go from?"

"Lotsa places. She didn't come the same way twice, that I remember."

"Me, too. Canny old dog, Well, sitting here jawing won't find them. Let's go."

Mom and Grace left the dishes on the sideboard and joined the search. They poked around the outside of the house very carefully—under the mesquite in the front yard, under the rock wall that held in the good dirt for the flower beds, under the house where the foundation was broken a little. No puppies.

Dan scoured the woodshed thoroughly, even moving a half cord of wood to see into the back corners. No puppies.

Pop checked every inch of the haymow. He gently lifted the hay forkful by forkful, listening for whimpering, feeling for weight. Daniel joined him, and together they searched the barn from front to back and top to bottom. No puppies.

How about the tool shed? No. Under the outhouse? No. In the springwash where tree roots hung out over the sand? No. Daniel and Pop walked the wash a few hundred yards in both directions. They encountered an upset gopher snake (Daniel really jumped; he thought at first it was a rattler). No puppies.

The rain had slowed down to a persistent drizzle when Daniel finally flopped into bed. He lay awake a long time thinking about Isobel and what she had cost already. He did not think of God at all until he had nearly dozed off. Carrie and Mom, who seemed to know a lot about God, were both confident the pups were safe in His care. Surely the pups would be all right until morning. Then Daniel would take up the search again, even more diligently. Before he finally drifted off to sleep, Daniel formulated a prayer to God to keep the puppies safe until they could be found. Confidence in God's providence crowded out his fear. He fell asleep.

Just after dawn the next morning the Carsons stopped by. They were going into Springer, and did Mom need anything from town? Daniel had already been up for an hour. It had stopped raining, but he was soaked anyway from lying on the ground to peek under things. When he saw Carrie in the wagon, he crossed the yard to say hello.

In piercing sopranos, Rachel and Naomi (Naomi still in her nightie) were simultaneously explaining the day before. Matthew, sitting by Carrie, mumbled hello, and Daniel returned his greeting.

Carrie smiled half-heartedly. "Rachel explained how Brown Bess got killed. Sort of. I'm sorry."

"We're looking for her pups. They're close by. We're sure of it."

"Can I help? I'd much rather look for puppies than go to Springer."

"You'd just get all wet and dirty. Look at me. Thanks anyway. They'll get hungry and start whining soon. We'll find 'em."

Carrie smiled, more warmly this time. "Well, Dan, rest assured that God is keeping watch over them."

Rachel tugged at Daniel's sleeve. "Danny, why is Isobel digging under the barn?"

"What?" Daniel turned and looked to where Rachel was pointing. Isobel was snuffing and snorting, rooting and pawing. She was making a small hole under the barn foundation into a bigger one.

A bright, hopeful thought lighted Daniel's brain. "Pop! Pop, come quick! Isobel's digging under the barn. Look how she's digging!"

The Carsons tumbled out of their wagon and gathered around the hole. Mom came running, and Pop came running with a shovel, He put his ear to the hole and listened. No sound. It was just a little hole, made by some badger long ago and recently widened. Or had Isobel widened it with her groveling?

Pop chipped away with the shovel. Isobel kept sticking her nose in and tried to bite Daniel when he held her back. Then Daniel flopped on his belly and reached in as far as he could. He did not stop to think that it was the perfect place for a rattlesnake den.

"How far back does it go?" asked Pop.

"I can't feel the end of it."

"Here. Move back." Pop scraped and spaded and widened the hole still more.

Daniel rolled aside as Pop pulled one boot off. Pop lay on his side and gently worked his long leg into the hole.

"Nice place for rattlesnakes," said Mr. Carson.

"Been thinking that very thing," said Pop. But he kept working his stockinged foot in farther. He grunted and turned red from straining. "Something in there. Can't feel just what. Think I've hooked onto it. There!"

Pop squirmed and started scooting backward, an inch at a time. Isobel stuck her nose into the action, and Daniel dragged her back again.

Pop pulled his leg out. His sock was soaking wet. He twisted around and reached in with an arm, his face tight and grim. He brought out the first pup, tiny and cold and stiff, and laid it beside him. It was all blond with a white face mark, just like Bess. There were two others that looked like Bess. The fourth was more like Zack, with the same mix of white, brown, and black.

They had found Bess's puppies, but so had the rain. Had she been alive, old Bess would surely have moved them when the water started coming in. Chilled and wet, they could not survive the cold night.

Daniel could not stop staring at them. He forgot the Carsons were standing around all glum. He forgot about Isobel. He forgot about Carrie until she laid a hand on his shoulder. Tears streamed down her cheeks.

Everything was piling up on him at once.

Daniel wheeled and screamed into Carrie's face, "So God is watching over them, is He? Well, Chet's right. You can keep your blooey about God. If God was paying any attention at all He wouldn't have let this happen. Your God's a phony, Carrie Carson!"

Daniel started running. He could hear Mom start saying something apologetic. Someone—Matthew?—called to him, and Pop said something to the caller. He kept running, back to the ten-acre bean patch, back to the hill beyond where it had all started. He ran nearly a mile before he collapsed, sobbing, on the crest of the hill.

The loss of Bess had emptied him. The loss of his final hope, her puppies, was even worse.

But what emptied him worst of all was this sudden, stunning flash of proof—this certainty—that Chet had been right all along. There was no God in heaven.

5

The Black Tornado

The whole summer went rotten. Everything about it left a bad taste in Daniel's mouth.

First there was Carrie. Daniel apologized to her a couple weeks later, and not because Mom told him he had to, either. He really was sorry he had clouded up and rained all over her like that. She accepted his apology graciously and expressed her own sorrow at the turn of events. But there was something strange between them now. The old, loose, easy friendship was gone. Carrie was less open, more distant somehow. She seemed to be thinking about other, deeper things. It disturbed Daniel.

Then there was Chet. Daniel had made a mistake mentioning Chet's lack of faith when he blew up there. Now his parents did not want him to associate with Chet at all. That restriction was easy enough to keep, though, because Daniel was too busy all summer to get over to Chet's anyway.

And work was a real drag. Homesteading was not nearly as glamorous in Texas as it had sounded back in Illinois. They had barely squeaked through the winter before, and this winter promised to be worse. Even little Naomi, now just turned four, was pressed into service now and then.

Pop's cotton patch dried up before the flowers turned to bolls. The javelinas got the beans. Twice. The grass along the river was so poor they were only taking off half the hay they needed. But it took just as much time to cut, ted, and haul the half-size cuttings.

Mom put up pitaya* preserves and prickly pear jelly, but then she had no time to braid straw hats for sale in Springer. The off gelding, Caesar, went lame from the lechuguilla, and they had to put up hay with only one horse. Rachel and Grace went out gathering candelilla† to boil down for wax and got lost for fourteen hours.

The most distasteful piece of work was the pen Daniel had to make. Without her friend and comforter, Bess, Isobel was making a royal nuisance of herself. She wallowed in Mom's flower beds out front and nearly got into the

---

*pih-TIE-ya; a strawberry-flavored fruit from a small cactus.

†candle-EE-ya; a jointweed, or ephedra, with waxy stems. Rendered, 100 pounds of stems yield 3 pounds of candle wax.

garden. She almost wandered off a couple of times. There was nothing for Daniel to do but pen her up.

She had turned into a truly moody pig now. Sometimes she would be all affectionate. Then she and Daniel could snuggle and play. More often, she would turn on him, bad-tempered. She bit him two or three times.

Daniel could not be too hard on her for that. He felt just like that himself—happy one minute and ready to bite the next.

It did not help the summer a bit when, one hot July night, Daniel got up to get a drink and heard his parents discussing finances. They were not actually arguing, but they sounded desperate. Even Pop was dismal. With no cash and little prospect of earning any, they would be lucky to keep food on the table over the coming winter. Any unexpected bills or illness would ruin them. Mom sounded especially bitter. When Pop said something about praying, and Mom replied, "To whom?" Daniel went quietly back to bed without a drink.

One of the biggest disappointments of the summer was church, and perhaps Mom's new attitude had something to do with it. She acted less certain that the good life began and ended in a church pew. Although the family still trooped off to services each Sunday, Mom had lost her staunch determination. And then, Rachel was going through a whining stage. Her whistle-blast whispers in church service were louder than some people's shouts, and other worshipers kept turning to stare. Grace was getting bossier, and she was always telling Daniel how to behave—usually during service. Naomi seemed more restless, constantly climbing all over him or falling asleep scrunched against him. Why did he always get stuck with Naomi?

Even his favorite part, the prayer-with-hymn, had lost its magic. It seemed useless. Why lift up your voice in prayer when the only god was between your own ears? And yet, Pastor Dougald was convinced he was talking to Somebody up there.

Daniel gave up trying to figure it all out. He would be observant, as Chet had long counseled. He would consider any additional evidence. But right now, the evidence pointed overwhelmingly the other way.

Toward the end of August most of the summer work was caught up, and the autumn work had not yet started. With a few hours free now and then, Daniel decided (after much deliberation) to go against his parents' wishes and visit Chet. He did not like being disobedient. In fact, he prided himself upon being "a good boy" most of the time. But the strictures against seeing Chet were unfair. Mom and Pop just did not understand Chet.

How should he go about it? He was not used to sneaking around behind his parents' backs.

He would have to be very careful. Let us see. He could take Isobel out for a walk and just keep on walking. That was it!

He would go out past the ten-acre bean patch and cut straight cross-country, across Tornado Wash. By going that back way he could get from his house to Chet's in less than two hours, visit half an hour or so, and get back home before supper. The whole distance covered would be less than one way by the road.

Friday morning he hurried through his chores, trying very hard not to look like he was hurrying. Then he climbed into Isobel's pen and tied the rope harness around her. She tried to bite him a couple times and drew blood once. This was not one of her loving days.

Neither was it Isobel's time of day for roaming. She and her kind start moving at dusk, not noon. Only mad dogs, Englishmen, and someone as crazy as Daniel would go traipsing across country on an August afternoon. She argued and squealed and hung back. She even sat down several times, to no avail. Daniel dragged her along even so.

It took a long time to get past the bean patch and over the ridge. Finally they were down the other side, still an hour from Chet's place. Before them stretched the broad, flat sand of Tornado Wash. Beyond the wash a vast white floodplain opened out, brilliant under the sun. Maybe Isobel had a point. Who would want to walk clear across that frying pan?

Suddenly, from the distance came the rumble of a galloping horse, approaching fast. Daniel did not know what to do. The brush was too low and sparce to hide in. He crouched behind a token creosote bush and gathered Isobel in close. She did not argue. She buckled her knees and squiggled into the dirt to rest.

The horse appeared around the far bend of the wash at a dead run. It was slim and black, the black intensified by the sweat glistening on its shoulders. With its nostrils flared out and its eyes rolled back it looked to Daniel just like the black horse of the Apocalypse. Daniel had never seen a horse running flat-out like that. He watched amazed and never thought to wonder why anyone would race a horse in this heat in this wilderness. The rider, crouched low, flicked the horse's shoulders with a riding crop.

And the rider was Chet!

Daniel stood up and yelled. He yanked his unhappy pig in motion, and they were well out into the wash by the time Chet had drawn his horse to a halt. The lathered beast loped back up the wash and Chet slid off next to Daniel.

"Hey, Dan! Good to see you! And hasn't that pig grown! Where have you been all summer?"

"Aw, lots of things happening. I'll tell you about it. Where'd you get that fantastic horse?"

"Pretty nice, eh?"

"Greatest I ever saw. And fastest."

"You bet! Hey, we have to keep walking. He'll get a chill and end up sick if I don't cool him out slow by walking him."

Daniel dragged Isobel along, and they ambled up the wide, sandy wash. Chet was so enthusiastic that he made Daniel feel great. The guilt about lying and sneaking past his parents vanished.

Chet explained. "I run him here because it's the only safe place to do it. No danger here that he'll step in a hole and break a leg. Badger holes, ground squirrel holes all over the place everywheres else. Even in Pa's bean field. Besides, running in loose sand strengthens his legs. When he hits a hard racecourse, he'll go like lightning!"

"What race course? Where will you race him, Chet?"

"Fair next month. County fair. And when he wins there I'll use the money to take him to the state fair."

"That's a far piece away."

"Worth going, if you have a winner. And I got a winner, Dan!"

"You sure do. But you didn't say where you got him."

Chet smiled knowingly. "Oh, picked up a little money here, a little there. Bought Tornado here (named him after the wash he runs in, right?) from some drunk over in Springer. The fellow didn't realize what he had. He was using

Tornado as a buggy horse, can you imagine that?"

No, Daniel could not imagine using the world's greatest racehorse to pull a buggy.

The world's greatest racehorse suddenly nickered. It was a curious neigh, the sound a horse makes when meeting a good friend. The boys glanced back. Tornado and Isobel were snorting, snuffing, touching noses. Isobel thrust her snout in the air and clicked her teeth with a happy squeal.

"Be careful!" warned Daniel. "She might bite him!"

Chet scratched his head. "Now ain't I a brass monkey! Looka that! No fear that either one of 'm will bite t'other."

Daniel shrugged. "It's your horse's nose. But this is the first time in two weeks that she hasn't felt like biting something."

Chet grinned. "Let's try a little something. Keep your pig here." He led Tornado down the wash a hundred feet, turned, and called, "Now give her some slack!"

Daniel let the clothesline out and gripped the end. Isobel shook her grizzled head and trotted off smartly—right to Tornado. Daniel joined Chet, and they continued their stroll through the sand.

"Now ain't that a marriage made in heaven!" Chet laughed. "I'm never gonna tell a soul about what we seen just now. I'd get locked up in the nut house fast . . . "

"No, you wouldn't. Nobody'd believe you."

"And lookit, Dan. Remember how nervous and jittery Tornado was just a couple minutes ago? Now he's as steady as a plowhorse. Ain't natural, but there you see it."

Indeed the horse was settled. He strode casually alongside Chet, his head low and ears wig-wagging. Isobel pranced beside him on her tiny staccato hooves, pressing as close as she dared.

The boys must have walked the wash a dozen times, talking and talking. Daniel did not notice at the time that he and Chet were equals—good friends without age, talking over old times. Daniel eventually took his leave and started back up over the ridge. He was filled with a strange mix of guilt and elation.

It was almost dark when Daniel got home. Rachel and Naomi were already in bed. Grace, pouting, was finishing the last of the chores—Daniel's as well as her own. Daniel finally decided the way out would be a downright lie. He told his folks he had gotten lost on the other side of Porksaddle.

And most deliciously frightening of all—inside him he held a secret, a big, compelling secret. Chet had drawn from him a sworn promise that he must never mention Tornado to a soul. Not a single person. Chet had a plan. He would keep Tornado a secret until the fair and the day of the race he had entered. No one would bet on a horse he knew nothing about.

Thus the betting odds against Tornado would be very high. Chet and his father would bet a large sum of money on Tornado and rake in a minor fortune when he won.

Daniel was scandalized and fascinated all at once. Gambling was one of those evils you never discussed out loud, especially at his house. It was a vice that no one you knew personally ever indulged in. And here was Chet, Daniel's best friend, talking about gambling and jacking the odds as if it were an everyday thing.

Life was becoming terribly complicated.

6

Brunhilde's Babies

Daniel visited Chet a couple times during the next few weeks, always in Tornado Wash. Chet was still exercising Tornado in the heat of the day, for the race would be run near 2:00 P.M. He spent hours carefully walking his horse out, rubbing its legs, doing all the things those rich eastern horsemen did. Sometimes Daniel would simply sit in the shade of a screwbean and watch, delighted.

On one of these visits, Isobel broke loose. Daniel had been careless tying her. Suddenly she was out in the wash as her friend came racing past. With her tail out rigid she did her best to match Tornado's strides. Her knobby little stick-legs were a blur. Chet laughed so hard he nearly fell off. Daniel had to sit down, so weak with laughter he could not chase Isobel.

But one short run down the wash was all Isobel's stamina could take. Tuckered, she curled up beside Daniel and slept away the remainder of the visit. After that the boys made sure she got her run with Tornado early on. Chet teased Daniel that he ought to enter Isobel also. Daniel returned the teasing by insisting he did not want to see Chet lose to a pig.

It was returning from one of these visits that Daniel saw cattle tracks in the dirt near the ten-acre bean patch. For a brief moment he panicked. The white bull was dead, gone for months, but . . . He noted, catching his breath, that these tracks were days old. He felt a little silly, becoming frightened of cow tracks.

The tracks reminded him of the bull, though. And he thought again of Matt. Except for church he had not even seen Matt all summer. If he were visiting Matt instead of Chet, his parents would not disapprove. He thought about how both those boys had changed since spring. He had not changed, of course. They had. Maybe his parents would get to know the new, real Chet, and then they would not disapprove.

His guilty feeling almost went away. But not completely. Sometimes it would surface to irk him as he lay in bed at night.

The last Sunday in August, Mom decided that they had all worked too long and hard to work still more on a Sabbath day. "Let's all go calling over to Carsons," she had said. So after church they went calling.

Daniel hated "going calling." It was not the same thing as visiting, and it was certainly nowhere near as nice as "dropping by." You had to speak properly and keep your tie on when you went calling.

It was too hot in the house, so everyone sat around on the porch. The smaller girls and boys ran off to play in the shade of the springhouse (Royal and Naomi got in a fight almost right away). Carrie, Daniel, and Matthew hung around with the grown-ups, mostly because no one could think of anything else to do in good clothes and a necktie.

As in every other August, conversation drifted around to the prospect of bringing in a schoolmaster for the winter. It had not happened yet in the two years Daniel's family had been in Texas, but the outlook this year was brighter (from the adults' point of view). In fact, maybe they could have a school open by October.

"After all," Pop pointed out, "just our two families here would put six children in the school."

"That's right," said Mr. Carson. "And when the three oldest get graduated out of eighth grade, Royal and Naomi will be starting."

"I don't know," said Carrie. "If I go off to normal school and learn to be a teacher, I'll have to stay in school longer than just eighth grade."

"That's true." Mom nodded. "What are your plans, Matt?"

Matt shrugged. 'I'm not certain yet, ma'am. I'm thinking about going into seminary. If so, I'd need more schooling than eighth grade, too. I do know that the Lord will lead me the way He wants me to go."

Now that hit Daniel. How could Matt be so certain? Matt had just said, "I know," without a bit of hesitation. It was the same as when he trusted God for help against the white bull. The same only different.

Then everyone was looking pointedly at Daniel. *What do you want to do when you grow up*? their eyes asked.

Daniel shrugged too. "Farming suits me all right." What do you say? Daniel had not given a moment's thought to his future.

Farming brought the conversation around to cotton prices, and Daniel quit listening. When Carrie wiggled a finger and left the porch, he followed. Anything was better than just sitting.

Carrie led the way into their barn loft. "I was going to surprise you, Dan, next month on your birthday. But I can't wait."

Daniel was startled to see Brunhilde, the massive, burly sheepdog, curled up in the hay. Bess could never make it up into their own loft. Then he realized Carsons' ladder slanted; Tremains' did not.

Brunny slammed her tail back and forth, a clumsy attempt at wagging it. Carrie parted the straw and lifted out a stubby bit of dark brown fluff.

"Here, Dan."

She dropped it into Daniel's hands. A puppy. It was maybe two weeks old; eyes open but not bright, mostly bulging belly and stubbed nose. All sorts of memories flooded his mind. Daniel felt tears coming and pushed them back. *Don't be stupid. There's a million puppies in the world.*

Daniel studied Carrie, and she looked back at him, her eyes steady. They were not staring each other down, just looking—for the first time in a long time.

"It's not Bess's, of course, but it has the same father. She's yours, if you want."

"I—I'll go ask Mom. Will Brunhilde mind if I borrow her?"

"Of course not. Right, Brunny?" Carrie sat down beside the oversize mother and scratched her neck. Daniel hurried down the slanting ladder with the brown pup and out to the Carson porch.

He waited politely until his mother was between sentences. Then he laid the puppy on her lap.

"Brunhilde's a mother, Mom."

"Isn't that a sweetie!" Mom lifted the pup to look it closely in the face.

Daniel let the puppy warmth soak into his

mother's hands and then continued, "Carrie says we can have her, if we like. When they're weaned, of course. It's not Bess's, but it's the same father."

Mom started to say something. But instead she got quiet, thinking. Daniel felt a nervous twinge. Mom chose her words carefully.

"We need a dog, very much, although this one wouldn't be much use until next spring at the earliest. Daniel, perhaps you'll consider trading off Isobel for this puppy."

Daniel did not catch it for a moment. Then his heart chilled. "What do you mean?"

"It's going to be a hard winter. We can't feed an extra mouth, Daniel. The pig is useless. Now the puppy here will grow into a fine watchdog. And Brunhilde is a good dog with animals—cattle and sheep both. I'm sure her herding instincts are inherited by this one. It will grow up into a useful, practical dog like Bess."

"What do you mean, 'trade off'?"

"Exactly that. The puppy would be yours. But we can't keep both animals over the winter."

"Now wait a minute, Martha." Pop was on Daniel's side—he just knew it!

"Ira, you know our situation as well as I do. Can you honestly say we can afford another mouth to feed?"

Silence.

Come on, Pop! Speak up! But he did not.

Instead, he took to studying a worn place on the knee of his Sunday trousers.

Daniel waited. The Carsons just sat around quietly, watching, looking self-conscious and a little embarrassed. Daniel took the puppy from his mother's hands without speaking. He walked back to the barn loft, up the slanting ladder into the dusty hay.

As soon as she saw him coming, Carrie asked, "What's wrong?"

"Nothing. We don't want a puppy just now, thanks. Not this year. Thanks anyway." He handed the pup off to Carrie, a bit too roughly perhaps, and hurried down the ladder. He could not keep back the tears any longer.

7

The Truck Garden

September 1 was not a hair cooler than August 31 had been, but saying the word "September" made it seem so. The first two weeks of the month, when Daniel would have started school back in Illinois, he now spent with his father on the road. They went out nearly every day gathering deadwood down along the river bottom. Long branches they kept as fence poles. The short and broken limbs they crosscut for firewood.

Caesar was still lame, but they had to use him. Cleopatra (who was also a gelding, but the name sounded good with Caesar) could not pull the wagon by himself when it was loaded. Caesar's painful limp kept them at a slow walk.

Daniel drove most of the time. While he handled the lines, Pop would bring out some whittling and work on wooden spoons for Mom or a limberjack for one of the girls for Christmas. He fashioned coat pegs and latches and triggers for deadfalls. Sometimes he mended harness or spliced rope.

Usually they rolled along slowly with only the creaking of the wagon and dry harness. Neither Pop nor Daniel was much of a talker. Sometimes, though, they got into lengthy discussions of this or that.

A couple times Daniel nearly told Pop about Chet's racehorse. But his new, close brotherhood with Chet kept him silent. He had, after all, promised. Besides, he still felt guilty—well, a little guilty—about lying to his folks and sneaking out. He felt guilty about keeping the secret from his father, especially since he wanted so badly to tell someone. And this God business bothered him most of all. There had to be a solid answer, and it kept eluding him.

One afternoon, as they were coming home from Blue Creek, Daniel just came right out and asked his father, "Pop? What do you think about God?"

Pop considered the question awhile. "Well, Dan—actually, that's more your mother's department. I don't think about Him much at all, really. Figure I'll let Him alone, and He lets me alone, and we're both satisfied."

This was a new one. Daniel had never thought of things that way. He ruminated a few minutes. Then, "What about gambling? Why is gambling wrong?"

"You planning on taking it up?"

"What would I bet on?"

"Good point. Bet there's gonna be a rough winter. You'll win. But then, nobody would bet against you on that."

"But why is gambling so wrong?"

Pop thought about that one, too, before he answered. Daniel liked that about him—he never gave Daniel second best, such as a thoughtless response.

"Gambling is wrong for a couple reasons, Dan. For one thing, it almost always takes money away from people who need it most and gives it to people who need it least. Usually crooks, at that. That's the worst as far as I'm concerned. And for another thing, the Bible speaks against it."

"But if you're letting God alone, what does it matter about the Bible?"

"Oh, now wait a minute, Dan. The Bible is a proven book."

"What do you mean?"

"You see, the Bible's been around for thousands of years, right? Now there's gotta be a reason for that. So you start looking around—"

"Being observant," Daniel cut in. Just like Chet was always saying.

"Right. Being observant. And you observe that the people who live closest to the Bible way of doing things get through life with the least amount of problems. Whether you're real religious like your mother or just stand back and let God go His way, you'll find the Bible is worth sticking with as a way of life. Can't go wrong."

"That's another thing. Mom doesn't seem as religious as she used to be somehow."

"Noticed that, huh? Ever since we dug them pups out she's been, well, reserved, sort of. I think you put some doubts in her mind, Dan, when you blew up."

"Sorry. I didn't think what I was saying."

"That's the whole point of it. If you'd been trying to hurt somebody's feelings it would have been different. We all know you weren't. You aren't the conniving sort anyway. What came out of you was honest anguish. And your Mom's been a mite troubled ever since."

"Carrie, too. Same way. Wish there was something I could say to set things right again with both of them."

"Maybe some day there will be. Something for you to say, I mean. Who knows?"

Daniel almost said, "God knows," but he caught himself in time. It nearly slipped out so naturally. Maybe he did believe in God after all. His pop did. You do not actively avoid someone you feel does not exist in the first place. Maybe this God business would work itself out yet.

Dawn. Well, not exactly. It was more like the half-light before dawn. Daniel burrowed into the quilts a little deeper, deciding whether it was worth waking up. As the sun rose later, so did Daniel.

Suddenly his mother's shrieks set him bolt upright. He grabbed his trousers and ran out the door barefoot. Something must be killing her!

Mom was out in the garden, half hidden by the fence rails. She was flailing about, swinging her broom. Pop fetched himself around the corner of the house at a dead run. His suspenders dangled below his waist, and his face was half shaved, half foamy with lather.

Isobel came squealing out the garden gate with Mom right behind. Mom looked bent on murder with that broom. Isobel knew better than to hide behind Daniel. She kept running. the fastest stiff-legged gait she could manage, past Dan and Pop, past the house, past the springwash. Daniel could hear the tiny cloven feet pattering across the dry sand behind the springhouse.

Daniel ran to the garden fence, afraid to look in. But you have to look eventually. And what he saw was the worst he could possibly see.

Every plant was rooted up. What she had not eaten, Isobel had trampled. She must have been carousing in there all night. There was nothing left. Nothing.

Mom appeared beside him and leaned heavily on the fence, her fury spent. Her face was dirty and tear-streaked. She had not cried when Bess got killed, but she was crying now.

Pop wrapped a lanky arm around her shoulder.

Her voice was a hoarse whisper. "It's all gone, Ira. Every bit of it. I don't think we can save a pint of vegetables out of it. Ira, what are we going to do?"

Pop was so livid with rage he was quiet. "Dan, go find out how she got out of her pen."

Daniel ran. When Pop was mad like this—quiet mad—it was worse than if he licked everyone in sight. It did not take Daniel more than a moment to find where Isobel had rooted and pawed and dug her way out under the pen rails.

Miserable, he hung back watching his folks. They were still looking at the garden. Then they turned slowly, Mom leaning on Pop, and walked to the house. The kitchen door closed.

Life was no longer just complicated and confusing. It was fast becoming unbearable.

Daniel forced himself to cross the miles of yard and acres of porch. He pulled open the leaden door and entered the kitchen. The girls were up, wakened by the noise. They cowered in the corner by the loft stairs, watching, listening, and in silent terror of their father's wrath. Even Naomi was afraid to make a peep.

Pop was still only half-shaved, but he had washed the lather off the other half. He was sitting at the table in his usual place. His voice was ice. "Sit down."

Daniel sat down.

"Dan, you know the garden was our edge. It meant the difference between surviving the winter and losing this farm—everything."

"Yes, sir."

"We don't have money to buy food all winter. We might even have to sell one of the horses if the hay gets too low. We couldn't afford to lose that garden, Dan."

"Yes, sir."

"What will we do about it?"

Daniel studied the knots in the flooring.

"Dan?"

"I don't know, sir."

"*I* know."

Daniel's head snapped up. Pop's eyes drilled into him.

"You're going to sell that pig for money to help get us through the winter. You won't get near as much for her as the garden was worth. But you'll get all you can. And if the chance comes along to find some odd jobs, you'll work for as much more money as you can get."

All the weight of the world pushed on his heart. "Pop, whoever would buy Isobel would buy her to butcher!"

"As I recall, that was one reason we kept her in the first place."

Pop sat back and softened a little. "I feel partly responsible, Dan. Your mom was right all along. We never should have taken Isobel in to start with. It's my fault partly, and I share the blame that things have come to this. But

Isobel is still basically your responsibility. There'll be no more said about this. Eat your breakfast. Then we'll go out and see what we can salvage from that mess."

Pop turned toward the stairs. "You girls, too. Get yourselves dressed, on the double. Hop to it!"

The girls ran like rabbits for the loft.

The next two days were the worst Daniel could remember, and he remembered the misery of leaving his friends in Illinois. Right after breakfast on both days, Mom left Grace to clean up the kitchen. For once Grace did not complain. She was too frightened. Rachel, Naomi, and Daniel took the south side of the garden. With their fingers they sifted through the trodden dirt for broken string beans and mangled pea pods. Most of the beet tops were eaten off, so Daniel turned over the beet rows with the potato fork as Rachel gathered the beets. They were small and slim, having achieved less than half their full growth.

Mom gathered the damaged kohlrabi, trimmed some leaves on the rest, and left them. Apparently Isobel did not much like kohlrabi. Pop propped up some of the cornstalks that looked like they might recover. He harvested the rest and muttered about the wisdom of cold-packing green corn.

By the first nightfall the family had gleaned most of what could be salvaged from the wasted garden, a few pecks at very best. It was a sorry supply to last a winter.

The whole next day was spent cleaning, preparing, and canning. The worst job was cleaning up the vegetables. Dirt was ground into everything. All the bruises and nibbled spots had to be cut away. Mom dug out the sauerkraut crocks and shredded the half-formed cabbage heads a leaf at at time. It was slow work.

Isobel showed up around noon looking for her dinner. She was in one of her rare lovable moods. Daniel could not stay angry at her as she nuzzled and rubbed. And he was sick at the thought of selling her for meat.

The problems that weighed on him—all of them: the God question, the hard winter coming, Chet and his secret racehorse and his gambling, Isobel—churned and churned in his skull. It was not until nearly suppertime that second day that the churning organized itself a little and a bright idea popped out.

The perfect solution! If only . . .

8

For Sale: One Pig

In a quiet way, Pop was very proud of his wagon rig. And no wonder. He himself had forged all the iron fittings and shaped the wooden pieces that made it convertible. It could be driven as a two-horse or even as a four-horse rig by the use of a tongue and singletrees, all detachable. Take the tongue off, and you could install shafts in a minute, converting the wagon into a one-horse buckboard sort of rig. Pop claimed the idea was not original. Lots of wagons were that way. What made him proud was that he had designed and built this one himself.

The pride rubbed off on Daniel as he drove the rig behind Cleopatra. It was a fine rig. He had tied Isobel close to the seat spring so she could not jump out of the back and be dragged. Oh, if only his idea would work!

Daniel had left home right after breakfast with the announced intention of selling Isobel, but he had not said where he was going. He hoped, he had said, to be back by suppertime.

The road around to Chet's place was hours longer than cutting cross-country through Tornado Wash. But since Daniel was officially out selling Isobel, he figured he ought to go about it officially, with the rig and road. Besides, he welcomed the extra time to think.

In fact, it probably would not do any harm to pray, just in case. Daniel thought a long time about what he ought to say to God—assuming God existed, of course—and how he ought to phrase his requests. But the final prayer, once composed and spoken aloud, was full of stammers and uh's and was only a few sentences long. Perhaps he had best leave that department to Pastor Dougald.

When Daniel drove into Chet's yard, he saw Chet's pa sitting on the porch, rocking. He did not stop to think how odd it was that a farmer should be taking his leisure at this time of day at this busy time of year. Chet's ma stepped out onto the porch, drying her hands on her apron.

She pushed some stray hair out of her eyes. "Why, looka here! Daniel Tremain, light, and set a spell."

"Thank you, ma'am." Daniel hopped down and wrapped a line around the porch rail, although Cleopatra would not go anywhere.

"I came to see Chet, if he's around. Business."

Chet's pa nodded. "He's down to the tobacco patch. We decided to spear it up early this year. Barton! You Barton! Run fetch your brother! Hit's business."

Barton waddled out from behind the chicken coop. He was even fatter now than when Daniel had last seen him. He scowled. "Aw, Pa, that's a quarter mile from here."

"That's right. That's why I'm a-sending you 'stead of me. So scat!"

Barton shuffled off under a grumpy cloud, hardly scatting. He was almost exactly Daniel's age, but Daniel did not chum about with him much. He was babyish and a general pain-in-the-neck.

Chet's pa came down off the porch. "So this yere's the famous musk hog. Chet tol' us all about 'r." He reached out and scratched the back of Isobel's shoulders. She was in her usual bad mood, but since that was her favorite scratching spot, she made no attempt to bite.

"How 'bout a drink, Dan'l?"

"Pa!" Chet's ma hissed. "They're church folks!"

"Know that. Coffee, o' course. How 'bout fetching this yere young man a cuppa coffee?"

Chet's ma went into the house, and Chet's pa went back to his rocker, so Daniel sat down on the edge of the porch. He looked around, amazed at how rickety a porch could be and still stand up. He thought of the stately farmhouses with their veranda-like porches—white fluted columns and carefully painted pickets—back in Illinois. They just did not compare with this ramshackle ramada of crooked mesquite poles and dry, weathered, porch planks.

Daniel squirmed a little, not certain what to say. But Chet's pa was ready to talk. "Chet tells me you're his best friend. Couldn't 've picked a better one, I say. He claims you're the only one he's told about his horse. He ain't even told Barton, least not everything. Barton knows he's racing, but he ain't never seen Tornado run."

"Fantastic horse."

"Surely so. Surely so. The fair's in two weeks, you know. Two weeks from yesterday, to be exact. We stand to make a peck o' money off'n that horse. Enough to get us through the winter and then some. Tobacco crop's real poorly this year. Not a leaf of cigar stuff in the whole patch. The cotton never did set bolls. Your pa have any luck?"

"Not with cotton or beans. We didn't plant tobacco." Daniel decided it was politic not to mention the garden at all.

"Then your cash crops are no better'n ours. Your pa's got it worse 'n me by a long shot. You know that? He only has you who's big enough to put in a full day's work. I got Chet, and Margaret's fourteen, and Barton's coming thirteen. I can hire 'm out, and that helps out a whole pile. Your pa can't hire out them sweet little sisters of your'n."

Daniel smiled. "Nope. Reckon Rachel and Naomi aren't good for too much yet. But Grace is a good worker, when she has to."

Chet's ma brought out a mug of coffee laced generously with cream and sugar. There was also a saucer with two muffins on it.

"Here y'go, Dan'l. The muffins are left over from breakfast. You can use'm."

"Thank you, ma'am."

Chet's pa was still talking, and Daniel had barely finished the muffins when Chet came around the barn and jogged up to the house.

"H'lo, Dan. What fetches you over so early?"

Barton was all ears, and Pa was not about to go away, so Daniel was forced to pretend he was grown-up. He would just have to talk to Chet man-to-man in front of everybody.

"Got a big problem, Chet. We have to sell off Isobel. Our crops are poorly, and we just can't afford to keep her over winter. We could butcher her, but Pop was thinking we need the money more than the meat. I mean, you see, we go fishing, and Pop sets deadfalls and snares when the weather's cool enough. So we get wild meat a-plenty.

"So, Chet, I was thinking how Isobel and Tornado take to each other so naturally. I was thinking you might want Isobel as company for Tornado, especially when you're on the road, like when you're racing in other parts of the state. You know how easy-going he is with

Isobel beside him." Then Daniel forced himself to add, "And if you really have to, you can always butcher her—if the winter gets too rough."

Chet looked all set to say no, but he paused. He smiled. He grinned. "Pa, fancy this: Here I come out onto the racetrack on Tornado, see? And while all those uppity, high-class racehorses have a pony beside 'm to keep 'm calm, Daniel here comes out leading Isobel. See?"

Pa snickered. "There's a flaw in your plan, boy. There wouldn't be no betting. Everybody would be falling off their seats laughing and breaking their necks."

Chet chuckled, "That's right! 'Specially nobody betting on Tornado. He'd be a laughingstock! Who would put cold, hard cash on a horse with a pig for a best friend? He'd look so stupid they'd try to take money off 'm!"

"If we thought the odds was sky high a minute ago, just lookit 'm now!"

"Ain't it beautiful, Pa?"

"And Tornado really does take to this yere musk hog, you say?"

"He does. They even run together. I never seen anything like it. 'Course, Isobel ain't no normal animal."

"Neither is Tornado." Chet's pa turned to Daniel.

"Dan, we're gonna buy your musk hog here for two reasons. No, three reasons. She'll be profitable to us in the way we just talked about. That is, she'll make Tornado look so foolish nobody'll bet on him. Jack the odds. And since you're Chet's best friend, hit's the least we can do for you. (Besides, hit's Chet who's more or less responsible for you having it in the first place).

"But mostly, hit's because I know your pa is gonna have a bad time this year. A real bad time. A lot rougher'n me. He'll need the money more'n I will."

Chet nodded. "Then all's left is to settle on a price. How much you asking, Dan?"

Daniel shrugged helplessly. "I don't have the least notion what a barnyard hog would bring, let alone little old Isobel here."

Chet's pa scratched his beard, a gesture designed to stimulate activity in his brain. "Well, let's see. Ten cents a pound would bring about four, five dollars. That is, when she's growed next spring, if not just yet. How does five dollars sound?"

Daniel went giddy with joy. He carefully adjusted his voice. "That's be just fine, sir!"

Chet's pa looked pointedly at Chet's ma. She wagged her head sadly and disappeared into the house. She came out presently with the sugarbowl minus its lid. Into Daniel's hand she counted out a dollar bill, three silver dollars, and loose change to bring the sum to five dollars.

Daniel folded the money up in his hanky

very carefully. He was so happy his hands shook. He was sure his face showed it, but he did not care. When he glanced up at Chet and his pa, they were grinning fit to split.

Chet's pa slapped his knee. "Business is done, and profitable business, too, for ever'-body. Ma, how 'bout some coffee all around, to celebrate."

Later, as Daniel was driving out of Chet's yard—without Isobel—he could hear Chet's pa talking loudly to Barton: "Now if you had any brains or guts I'd send you out to do business like Dan'l there. He don't mope around all day complaining; he gets out and hustles. Same age you are, and he's a man already. Why can't you be like Dan'l?"

And the voice faded past hearing. That was just the way Mom was always talking to Daniel about Matthew. "Why can't you be more like him?" Daniel knew for a fact that he himself was not a model worth imitating. Particularly, he was not to be considered a man yet. Could it be that Matthew was human, too?

9

Spilling the Beans

Cleopatra plodded down the dusty track, his neck stretched out, his head bobbing. He could sleep walk, a gift Daniel envied many a time. Daniel had told Mom he would try to be back by supper. Here it was not quite one o'clock yet. And there was one more item of business to attend to. With difficulty, Daniel wrenched Cleopatra's head away from home direction and steered him down the side road toward the Carsons'.

It was almost four when he drove into Carsons' yard. Brunhilde bounded out at a floppy gallop. The huge dog knew Daniel and Cleopatra as well as she knew her own family. Daniel sat in the box a few moments, waiting for her enthusiasm to wane before he climbed down. She often knocked him over in the first flush of happy greetings.

Out in the side yard Carrie was pouring a batch of soap into flat tin pans. Her sleeves were rolled up for good reason—she was splotched in grease all the way to her elbows. Like Daniel's mom, Carrie looked especially pretty when she was hot and sticky from working.

Matthew came over from the woodshed, stripped to the waist, the splitting maul still in his hand. He gave Daniel a warm grin and a handshake. Daniel considered that very charitable of him, since he was several years older.

"The folks are in town today. Ma's selling off some of the chickens. They'll be back by supper. Stay and eat with us."

"I'd like to, Matt, but thanks. I just stopped by to see how the pups are doing."

Carrie came running over, laughing. "Oh, you've got to see them! Come on."

Matthew grinned. "Follow Carrie. The pups are her department." And he returned to his woodsplitting.

Carrie led Daniel not to the loft but to the lean-to tacked to the barn.

"We had to move them down here. We were afraid they'd tumble out of the loft. You can't believe how clumsy they are!"

They stepped into shadowy darkness. Daniel's eyes required a minute to adjust. The pups, not quite ready to wean, had grown tremendously. They were playful now, too—at least the ones that were awake. They waddled about on huge paws, all bandy-legged. One clawed its way up into Daniel's lap uninvited. It was the dark brown one Daniel had held weeks ago.

"Sure is a difference, Carrie. I forgot how fast pups grow." He hesitated. Then, "Uh—any of them still need a home?"

Carrie's face fell. "I'm sorry, Dan. They're all spoken for. In fact, we have so many offers we're selling, not giving them away. 'Course we surely wouldn't have asked any money from you folks. I guess everyone wants a big herding dog like Brunny."

"Sure, No doubt. Brunhilde's a valuable dog. Her pups ought to be just as fine. Bet Ramon Guirran's buying one."

"Two." Carrie forced a giggle. "Well, they all inherited Brunny's grace and poise. They even fall in the dog food dish. Now if only they've got some of her herding savvy . . ."

Daniel scooped the hefty brown pup off his lap and stood up. "Sure wish I could stay longer, but I told my folks I'd be home for supper. Just stopped a minute since I was passing by anyway."

"Well, you won't make it home by supper. Why not just stay and eat with us? You'll be taking a chance, of course. I'm cooking. But you're welcome."

"Thanks, Carrie. I'll be home quick enough. Cleopatra always moves faster homeward than outward."

"Don't they all."

They stepped, squinting, into the bright sunshine and wandered slowly toward Cleopatra.

"How's Isobel?"

"Doing fine." Daniel decided to say no more. How do you explain why Chet would buy her, without spilling Chet's secret?

Suddenly, Carrie asked, "Dan? You still think God is a phony?"

Daniel shrugged. "I don't know. I've been thinking about that a lot lately. Soon's I about make up my mind, something happens to make it look some other way. I just don't know. Has—uh—Matthew said anything about it?"

Carrie nodded. "He has. He says faith is like raising a crop of wheat. First you plant the seeds. That's believing in God. But it's just the beginning. The seeds have to sprout, and that's believing in the Son of God, Jesus. Then the grain filling out, that's the way of life that grows out of being committed to Jesus. Bible calls it the fruit. Finally, then, the harvest is where you get your rewards and go to heaven. And you can't skip any one step. Not any more than a stalk of wheat can skip a step and amount to anything."

"Sounds like Pastor Dougald, sort of."

"But easier to understand. Matt has a gift for that."

"Yeah, but that first step, planting the seed. Believing in God. How do you find out for sure that there is a God to believe in?"

Carrie stopped and stared at the dirt. Daniel

could tell she was not avoiding him. She was just thinking, her forehead all wrinkled. "You know, I don't know, Dan. Matt is so sure God exists, and so is Ma, that it never occurred to me that He might not. At least not until you dug those pups out. My big problem's always been—well, does God really care about anything, like your puppies. Maybe He's too big, important and busy to bother with pups or you, or me—or this whole world."

They stopped at the wagon but somehow Daniel did not feel ready to leave yet. They stood around, waiting.

Carrie snapped her fingers. "Dan, I just thought. People have been worshiping and being religious for thousands of years, right? Not just Christians and Jews, but everybody. All people, everywhere. If there weren't any God, I don't think that could be. Not as much as it is, I mean—you know what I mean?"

Daniel brightened. "Yeah! All over the world, the same thing. There's gotta be something to it." He glanced at the sun. It was hovering close to the horizon—much too close. "Look how late it is! I gotta go. See you soon, I hope. And say hello to your folks."

"I will. Oh, here. Wait a minute."

While Daniel climbed onto the box, Carrie ran into the house. She came out a moment later with a quart canning jar. "Ma made apple butter yesterday with the first of the green windfalls. I know she wanted you folks to have some."

"Hey, thanks. Mom'll appreciate that. Well. Later."

"Later."

Carrie stood watching as Daniel hauled Cleopatra around and pointed him homeward. Just before he passed the mesquite clump that would screen the house from view, Daniel glanced back. Carrie was still standing there.

Daniel got home later than he expected, but Mom had supper waiting for him. Pop was outside finishing up chores, and the girls were in bed already, all of them. It was not quite bedtime, but they had been whining and moping over the loss of Isobel, and Mom was sick of hearing them, she said.

All Mom asked him was, "How'd you do?" and he said, "Fine." Mostly he was too hungry to talk. Except for those two muffins at Chet's, he had had nothing to eat since breakfast. He did find space between mouthfuls to tell about his visit to the Carsons'—and that there were no longer any puppies available.

When Pop finally got in, Mom had his place set with coffee, fresh bread, and Carsons' apple butter. Pop did not bother to say hello. His first words were, "Well, how'd you make out?"

"All right." Daniel kept it as casual sounding as he could. The most exciting part of the whole day was fast becoming this part right here—where he was sitting like this with Mom and Pop, talking not as a child to grown-ups but as one person to another. A year ago he could not have imagined conversing with them as an equal.

He opened his hanky up and dumped his money out onto the middle of the table. The silver dollars gave a nice ringing sound.

"My land sakes!" Mom gasped. "Who would think that a wild pig would bring . . ." She stirred through the coins quickly. "Why, that's five dollars. I can't imagine that!"

Pop laughed. "You must've talked like a Philadelphia lawyer! Now you gotta tell us who'd you take across for all this money?"

"Chet's pa."

Mom turned cold, and Pop sank back some. "I wouldn't have thought that wily old buzzard would pay a nickel for a javelina."

Daniel sat silent, all confused. Should he speak out or should he not? Would standing up for Chet's pa destroy this fragile equality with his parents?

Mom said, "Well, money's money and a deal's a deal, regardless who made it. But Dan, how'd you talk them into paying so much for an animal they can go out and get for the price of a bullet?"

Daniel tried to rake his thoughts together, but the confusion in his head kept his tongue tied up. He must have sat there longer than he intended.

Mom pushed him. "Dan, I asked you a question."

"Now wait a minute, Martha. Can't you see he's sifting things out? I smell something bigger'n a javelina here. Am I right, Dan?"

"Yes, sir. A lot more, Pop. First there's Chet's family. All you two ever do is complain about them. The way you talk, they're dirt. But Pop, do you know that one of the big reasons they bought Isobel was because they're worried about you?"

"About me?!"

"You don't have any working-age kids except me, and Chet's pa has three . . ."

Mom snorted. "He'd have four if he'd just get off his backside and work a lick himself."

Daniel kept going. "And he says your winter is going to be a lot rougher than his, and you'll need the money. Pa, he *cares* about us! And you don't care a fig for him or his. He calls us church-going folks, and we don't even say hello in return. We never even thought about their winter."

Mom looked at Pop with a strange, hurt sort of look on her face. Pop rubbed his chin.

" 'Nuther thing," Daniel pressed on, "I promised Chet I wouldn't tell a soul, but I can't just sit still without telling you. He has a horse he's gonna race at the fair. His family is betting a pile of money on him, and they're keeping how fast the horse is a secret . . ."

Pop cut in. "So the odds will be higher, right?"

"That's right. And one of the reasons they bought Isobel is because she and Tornado are friends. She's company for him to keep him from getting all flustered."

"Tornado's the horse, I take it."

"Now wait!" Mom burst in. "Horses and wild pigs don't mix. The notion's ridiculous."

"This horse and pig mix, Mom. You see, once in a while Isobel and I been walking over to Tornado Wash, and that's where Chet works his horse out. They took to each other. Even run together some. Besides, Isobel will make Tornado look stupid so the odds are even higher."

Mom was absolutely grim. "I see. That explains a great deal."

"How fast is this horse of Chet's?" Pop asked.

"He's really something, Pop!"

"Well, he's gonna have to be. I hear there's some fellow over at Brewster County Fair this week who's racing his horse, and he's coming to our fair next week. This fellow, he makes his living racing the fair circuit. It's a fancy, professional racehorse like they run on the eastern tracks. He runs against local horses and really cleans up. Nobody's beaten him yet."

"Tornado'll give him a good run, Pop."

"What if Tornado doesn't win?"

"He will. You should see him."

Pop drained his coffee and glanced over at Mom for a refill. Suddenly he grinned. "Dan, I admire your savvy. That's the only place in the whole world you might sell Isobel without sending her straight to the butcher block. Clever. Mighty clever."

"I don't see anything clever," Mom said. "Lying to us, sneaking around behind our backs to do something he knew he shouldn't."

"I'm sorry, Mom. I really am. I been feeling guilty ever since I first did it. That's another thing's been bothering me. Chet and I—well, he's my friend, and I won't apologize about him. But I feel guilty about lying, and I'm sorry."

Pop looked steadily at Mom as he said, "Since you're truly sorry, you're forgiven, Dan. We'll forget it and say no more about it. Now. Anything else preying on your mind?"

"Well—uh—sort of. But it's philosophical sort of stuff. I'll work it out I think."

"Dealing with gambling or with God?" Pop still remembered that conversation from weeks ago!

"God mostly."

"Might have a chat with Matthew. He knows the bushes where you can pick the best berries in that department."

"Matt. Yeah, I might."

Mom asked, "Anything else?"

"Yes'm. Is there any more apple pie left?"

10

County Fair

Braaaang, budludludl bambambambang braammma braaammma. The firehall marching band, followed closely by the almost-new pumper-ladder rig, looked splendid. Each member was decked out in a bright red shirt, black trousers, and the suspenders of his choice. And they sounded almost as good as they looked. The horses, of course, were equally magnificent with polished brass hames and red yarn in their manes. The bass drum made Daniel's breastbone thump a bit as it passed.

The parade through downtown Springer was the traditional opening of the county fair, and Daniel's family never missed it. There were sometimes parades on Independence Day or some other notable occasion, but the band saved its best stuff for this one.

Merchants strung out banners, and the street department whitewashed all its rolling stock. Everyone celebrated the opening of the county fair.

Daniel's family watched the parade from a vantage point next to Grant's Mercantile. Pop set Naomi up on his shoulders. Daniel could remember long ago when Mom carried baby Grace in her arms and he sat on Pop's shoulders. After the parade Pop announced that they would visit the fair one day only. There was no money to spend on things like fair junk and too much work to do on the farm.

Mom brought some of her canned vegetables, just in case (there was a modest cash prize for the top winners in the home-canning division). Pop complained about selling Isobel. She would certainly have placed first in her division at the swine show. It took Grace quite a while to realize that Isobel would have been the only entrant in her division, being the only tamed javelina in the county.

Mom traded some fertile eggs for white sugar, and the merchant insisted on candling every one of them before he would surrender the sugar. Daniel's cheeks burned for his mother's sake.

Around noon Daniel's family bumped into Chet's family. To Daniel's considerable surprise Pop invited them to join the Tremains for a picnic lunch. Mom and Chet's ma picked the picnic site, a cool wash just beyond the fairgrounds. They all walked out there (Naomi whining the whole way) and spread the picnic cloths under a mesquite clump.

The ladies and small children sat in the shade of the stunted mesquites. Pop and Chet's pa ate lunch in the shade of a nearby ocotillo*, which is the same as no shade at all. So Chet and Daniel loaded their napkins with fried chicken and potato salad and sat off by themselves.

Chet grinned, fried-chicken-grease glistening on his chin. "Isn't the weather perfect, Dan?"

"Little on the hot side."

"That's right! Tornado's used to running in weather hotter than this, but that mystery horse ain't. He's been running mostly up north."

Daniel smiled. "Things are looking pretty good all around, aren't they?"

"Sure are! The word's out about that other horse and just *no*body's betting on Tornado. The odds are bigger than we coulda hoped."

"That's great, Chet."

"Surely so. Say, tell me, Dan. How much've your folks put on Tornado?"

"None."

"Hey, come on!"

"Not a dime, Chet. Honest. Pop and Mom neither one hold with gambling."

---

*Oh koh TEE yo; a woody desert plant with straight, spiny stalks growing up in a spray from a stocky base.

"Dan, this ain't gambling. Hit's a sure thing."

"Chet, you ever see this other horse?"

"I've seen Tornado." He scooped up another bite of potato salad. "No money at all?"

Dan shook his head, suddenly embarrassed by his parents' straitlaced ways. He concentrated on his chicken drumstick.

Chet leaned over and poked him. "Why don't *you* put down some, then?"

"Me? I don't have any money."

"I know at least five dollars you got. Know what the odds are? Forty to one. Forty to one, Dan."

"That high, huh?"

"You put down your five dollars, you pick up two hundred dollars. That's how high."

Daniel stopped in mid-bite, staring. Two hundred dollars! Then he shook his head. "It's not my five. It's the family's. No, I couldn't. Really."

Chet shrugged. "Well, you best to change your mind before tomorrow afternoon. Soon as the horses step out on the track, the betting's closed."

"I'll—uh—think about it, Chet."

"Knew you'd get smart quick." Chet sat up straight. "Hey, Ma! Any potato salad left?"

After lunch the two families walked back to the fairgrounds and then split up into small, wandering knots. Mom and the girls wanted to walk around the grounds looking—not to spend money, mind you—just looking. Pop decided to go check out the cattle and swine—milk cows mostly.

There were no races on the first or last days of the fair, so Chet and his pa would bring Tornado in tomorrow morning. Daniel wandered down the rows of horse stalls, peeking into identical semidark compartments to look at identical bay horses. He asked around, but the mystery horse had not come in yet either.

Daniel, who had been so excited about the fair that morning, suddenly found it disturbing. That business about gambling, the promise of $200, sort of spoiled it. He did not want to be at the fair anymore. He went off looking for either Pop or Mom and found Mom first.

There were some picnic leftovers for supper, but not much. Maybe Daniel might catch some fish, and they could stop along the road on the way home to eat fried fish and corn dodgers. "Fine," Mom said, "but are you sure you would rather go fishing than see the fair?" Daniel was sure. He took his pole and doughballs from the wagon and walked over the hill to Springer Mill Creek.

Daniel was planning to drop his line into an abandoned millpond, but someone with the same idea was there ahead of him. He was about to walk farther downstream when he recognized the other fisherman. It was Matt. Might as well join him. Matt would not mind.

Matt glanced up. "Hi, Dan!"

"H'lo. How's it going?"

"Nothing. This was going to be our supper, too."

Daniel grinned, "Us, too. Why don't they ever bite when you need 'm?"

Matt waved a hand. "Well, sit yourself down and join me. We can watch the worms drown together."

Daniel plopped down and dug out a doughball. They were pretty old and ripe, all the better for luring bullheads and suckers. He fiddled around a long time getting his hook into the water. He felt agitated and nervous for some reason. He cleared his throat.

"Uh, Matt, been meaning to talk to you. Pop's idea. But the time never came up. We've been pretty busy."

"So've we. Every day there's something else to do and never enough time to get it done. Anything in particular you want to talk about?"

Daniel, in a way, had looked forward to talking to Matt, but somehow he had never pictured it as happening this way. He felt terribly uncomfortable. Well, since it was happening this way, he might as well get it over with.

"Got a question. A couple months ago you said you were sure God would lead you, and you sounded so certain. How could you be so sure?"

Matt grinned and drew his line in. The cork out there leaned toward shore and bobbled at them, leaving a thin V-line wake behind. As Matt rebaited his empty hook he explained. "Well, Dan, it didn't just jump out and grab me one day. When I was about your age (you're the same age as Carrie, aren't you?), I got to thinking about God, and I felt all confused. I mean, here were folks going to church every week, but what was the use of it? Know what I mean?"

Daniel sure did!

Matt flicked his line back out into the flat, still water. "So one day I was talking to Pastor Dougald. I recall I was mad about something—really truly mad—but I can't remember now what it was. Anyway, we talked for an hour. He didn't tell me what to believe—he just set me thinking in the right direction. And reading the Bible. Since then God has been showing Himself to me in ways that prove to me He exists. And that He loves me."

And that He loves me. This was another new element to Daniel. The pastor preached love sermons every now and then, but Daniel had never considered such love on a one-to-one basis. But he did not think too much about that because mostly he was thinking, *Why does Matt use a cork for bullheads and suckers?* Then he decided that Matt, always the optimist, might be hoping that something a little better than catfish and suckers was out there. Matt was usually looking toward something a little better—and usually finding it.

"All right. So what direction did the pastor get you to thinking in?"

Matt forgot about watching his cork. He was concentrating on Daniel now. "My problem was, I was expecting God to wave His big hand in front of my face to prove Himself. You know, like He proved Himself before Elijah and the prophets of Baal. But the Scripture says, 'Seek ye the Lord while He may be found.' I had to do the searching myself without expecting God to do all the work. Like the pastor said: Men say, 'Prove it, and then I'll believe.' But God says, 'Believe, and then I'll prove it.' "

Daniel felt frustrated—the answer had seemed so close, and now it was not. "But how can you believe in God when He doesn't even bother to prove Himself to you?"

"I didn't say that. He did prove Himself. *After* I accepted Him. Look here. If you see evidence that God exists, and you analyze it, and so you believe, where's your faith?"

"In God."

"Nope. In your own ability to read the evidence right."

"Yes, but—"

"Look again. Let's say the evidence proves God does not exist. Like when you lost those puppies last June. You see the evidence, and you say, 'God doesn't exist.' But what if God really does exist, except that He intended the puppies to be a lesson for somebody else? I mean, there was a whole flock of people there standing around. Maybe the puppies had nothing to do with you at all. Maybe you were mistaking a lesson God intended for one of us Carsons. You read the evidence wrong, then, see?"

"You think that's really the way it was, Matt?"

Matt shook his head. "No, I think just the opposite. I was just using that as an example. I think the puppies were meant to help you and your folks find God."

The memory of the four stiff, cold little bodies came back strong. "Don't you think He could've picked some better way?"

"Maybe. Maybe not. God knows you better than I do. I was just pointing out that you can't trust yourself to read the evidence right about whether God exists. Remember when Jesus said a sparrow couldn't fall without Him knowing? Fall, Dan. He didn't promise to keep the sparrow up in the air."

"You mean whether it lives or dies, it's God's."

"You got it!" Matthew turned, settled back, and finally paid some attention to his cork.

This was the strangest feeling. Daniel was certain he had just learned a lot, but he could not for the life of him say what it was he had just learned.

Matt's cork bobbled and disappeared. Matt set the hook gently and drew in his catch, a small sunfish. "That's one." He rebaited and sent the line back out.

Daniel sighed. "Then I'm worse off than before. Even if God tries to prove Himself I might not catch it. How do you ever know anything about God at all?"

"Ah, now we're getting to faith!" Matt was getting excited. In fact, he was becoming even more enthusiastic than Chet had been when first telling Daniel about his horse-racing plans. Matt again abandoned any interest in his cork. "Look, Dan. Let's say I build a milkstool out of good oak and set the legs solid, and then I sit on it. No faith there. I know it's going to hold me. But let's say Royal gives me a milkstool he just made. If I sit on it without checking it over, I'm really stepping out on faith—faith that Royal didn't try to stick the legs to the bottom with library paste."

"Royal builds things that way."

"He sure does. You should see the birdhouse he came up with last week. Five walls."

"I don't get the faith thing."

"God is trustworthy. But I don't know that to start with because I don't even know for sure He exists. So I take a step of faith. I say, 'All right, God, I'll believe You are who You say You are.' Through the Bible, that is. Disregarding what you think the evidence is."

"But that's blind faith. Isn't Pastor Dougald always saying you shouldn't depend on blind faith?"

"Right! You don't stay there, it's just where you start out. The great thing is, once you express faith, then God has something to build on. And He does build on it. Unless you neglect it, your blind faith doesn't stay blind."

Daniel stared at him. "Man says, 'Prove it and then I'll believe,' but God says, 'Believe and then I'll prove it.' "

"I just said that a minute ago."

"I know. But I didn't understand it then."

Matt's eyes were shining, his face glowing with the happiness of sharing something really fine. "Then the second step is accepting Jesus in the same way. To be a believer is simply to believe Him."

"Yeah. Carrie told me about the wheat thing. One step at a time."

Matt nodded. "Good. Start out by accepting that God and Jesus are who they say they are whether you're sure or not. That's faith. Then read your Bible, and you're on the road. The more you step out on faith to a new level, if you know what I mean, the more your faith grows and the more real God becomes to you."

Daniel sat back and buried himself in thought. It was too simple to be true, and yet it was the deepest thing imaginable.

Matt caught a couple more sunfish, pulled the cork off his line and went after bottom-feeders. The boys fished nearly an hour more and eventually had enough on the string to feed both families.

Daniel had been hearing "salvation" his whole life. This was the first moment he actually realized what the word meant. Then everything just sort of fell into line. He and Matt put together a prayer asking that Daniel be forgiven of all his sins. They asked Jesus to take over for him and direct his life—to just step in and guide him when he needed it. And Daniel finished by saying, "Thank You." His turmoil over the God question was suddenly gone. Daniel felt very much embarrassed about the tears in his eyes until he saw Matt's eyes. And Matt was two years older than he was, too!

That night on the long drive home Daniel considered telling his parents about this Jesus business. But they were up in the box, and he was in back with the girls. The girls were asleep on straw ticks, and Daniel did not feel very much awake himself. Without even trying, he fell asleep thinking not of Isobel, nor of Chet and Tornado, but of Jesus.

11

The Race

Dawn, or nearly so. Junior Goose, the rooster, was announcing it a little early. Daniel lay in bed thinking—if he was going to do it he must do it now, before his parents woke up. It was wrong to go against your parents' wishes. But then, what if they were wrong?

Jesus was watching over his shoulder. But Jesus wanted the family to prosper as much as anyone did. You cannot just ignore $200!

Daniel got up and dressed quietly. Carrying his shoes he crept down barefoot into the kitchen. Where would Mom keep the money?

He remembered that Chet's ma had kept hers in a sugar bowl. By stretching on tiptoe he just barely reached the sugar bowl. It was full, all right—of sugar. Try again.

Beyond it on the top shelf was the cracked teapot, useless but too pretty to throw away. Daniel stood on a chair and lifted the teapot down. There it was—his five dollars. Well, the family's five dollars, actually. No, five dollars and sixty cents. Mom had sold some eggs.

Daniel left the sixty cents. You could probably only bet whole dollars anyway. He wrapped up the money and stalked silently out of the house into the chill September dawn. Then he started running. He wanted to make it to Springer before the races started. He did not know exactly which race Tornado was entered in.

It was strange being at the fair alone—Daniel had never entered the gates without his family before. He was afraid he might have to pay part of the five to get in—why had he not brought the sixty cents? But his Mom's entry in the canning division gave him free access.

The fair was an exciting place, every corner of it. But Daniel headed straight for the track and stables. A couple of harness horses were already parading onto the track. Fair officials were trying harness racing this year for the first time, the kind of racing so popular back on the Eastern tracks. Daniel had grown up in Illinois knowing nothing but trotting and pacing purses, but out here, of course, everything was different. Daniel paused to watch the second heat of a trotting purse.

Most of the racers were homegrown, but two of the drivers wore fancy silk shirts and high laced boots. The sulkies were so light they bounced a bit on the rough track. *Bet you could go a mile a minute in those sleek little rigs!*

Daniel stood at the outside rail on the first curve. Apparently not too many fair patrons were interested in sulky races. The bleachers were just beginning to fill, at five cents a head.

Daniel had never seen such a sloppy moving start before. The horses came around the far turn within about ten feet of each other. "A fair start!" the announcer shouted into his megaphone. The horses bore down on Daniel and the first turn. He almost flinched as one swung wide and broke stride. The horse's sweat flecked onto Daniel, he was so close. The driver was pulling so furiously to the left that the horse's jaw was wrenched out of line. Dinner-plate hooves slammed solidly into the dirt. The driver never did get out of last place.

Horseracing was beginning to look a lot more exciting than farming. Maybe Chet could use an assistant.

As the trotters drove home, Daniel managed to see the racing card of the gentleman standing next to him. Tornado and the mystery horse were both in the next race.

Well, this was the time. Daniel would have to do it now. Take his five dollars to the stand behind the bleachers, trade it for a small ticket—and then throw the ticket away if Tornado did not run well.

And in the middle of it all was the constant thought of Jesus—Jesus as Daniel had seen his picture in a book, with the yellow ring around His head and a sad look on His face. Two hundred dollars! And God's countenance no longer shining upon him. Enough money to get us through the winter and extra seed for spring planting. It is not for me—it is for Mom and Pop, every penny.

The megaphone voice announced the second race to the people in the stands. The people back in the stables already knew it. Horses, men and boys were churning about like popcorn in a pan. Tornado was in the midst of them, sidling and pawing. And so was Isobel. Chet had enlisted Barton as pig handler, and Daniel was glad. Fat old Barton looked even goofier than Daniel would have, and that was the whole idea.

Daniel was elbowing through people to reach Chet when he saw the mystery runner. He stopped cold, awed. The horse was at least two hands* taller than Tornado, slim and perfectly muscled. Its neck arched proudly. Here was a sleek, chestnut-colored running machine born for the sole purpose of winning races. Obviously the horse was accustomed to crowds. Whereas it moved about with a quiet disdain,

---

*That is, eight inches higher at the shoulder.

Tornado was in a lather of nervous fear already, Isobel or no Isobel.

The chestnut's rider was just as professional as his horse. He wore fancy Eastern racing silks and used a special saddle barely more than a leather pad with stirrups. The horse was fitted with a pair of cup-like blinders at its eyes, the better to keep it running true. This fellow was equipped with every scientific device!

It suddenly, painfully occurred to Daniel that Tornado might not be the world's greatest racehorse after all. O God, what would Chet's pa do if they lose?

Well, Matt had told him prayer was very important. Trying not to look conspicuous, Daniel closed his eyes briefly and prayed. Since God already knew the situation he did not take time to review it. He simply asked God, hastily, to help Chet win.

The first three entrants paraded onto the track amidst cheers. Daniel got close enough to Tornado to yell good-luck greetings to Chet. Chet grinned weakly in return. He was clearly as nervous as his horse. Barton looked intensely uncomfortable. His embarrassment and the noonday heat together made his shiny red face even redder.

Tornado stepped out on the track the next to last. He was the shortest, stockiest horse there. Somehow Daniel had not noticed his small size when he was running alone in Tornado Wash.

And how the crowd roared as Isobel came mincing out beside him! They roared louder as Tornado thrust his blocky nose down, and the two friends touched, just to reassure each other than these crowds were a dream, and all was well. Isobel was performing like a circus star.

Well, Chet's plan had worked. No one in his right mind would bet on that balmy black animal! Then the mystery runner was out on the track last of all, striding in stately confidence.

Daniel looked up into the bleachers and at the railbirds all around him. There were lots of people here now, probably to see that big chestnut run. He glanced behind him, too. And there was a familiar, lanky figure lurching through the crowd, searching. How could Pop have known?

Daniel briefly considered running, but it was too late. Pop had seen him. There was no way out now. Daniel slouched by the rail and studied a small tuft of grass that had survived the summer by huddling against the railpost.

As usual, Pop did not bother with hello. "We checked the teapot first thing, soon as we saw you were gone."

Daniel did not have to ask how Pop had managed to get there so fast. He saw the horse sweat and the bay horsehairs on the seat and legs of Pop's trousers. He had ridden Cleopatra in, and at a good clip too.

The megaphone barked, "Fair start!" Pop and Daniel both spun around to watch the track.

Tornado was running well today. He almost took the lead. But then the mystery horse was in front and in front to stay, it seemed. The ground rumbled as three tons of horses pounded past in a dense pack.

Pop asked, "Mile or half-mile?"

"Mile. Twice around."

"Tornado was only running half-mile heats in that wash, wasn't he?"

"Yeah. And Chet never rode in a real race before."

Pop grimaced. "That's obvious. The boy don't know the first thing about finding that inside rail."

On the backstretch the pack opened up a little. The horses bunched again on the far turn. They churned past the grandstand in an opaque cloud of dust. The crowd howled and stomped.

Tornado was fourth now. As they passed Daniel and his father the second time, Tornado was finally edging against the inside rail. Chet huddled against his horse's neck, leaving the reins fly loose. He had turned the race over to Tornado!

The local horses dropped back one by one, and Tornado was second. Daniel started yelling at Chet to lay on the whip, one small voice among hundreds.

On the backstretch Tornado started moving, his ears flat against his head. He got within ten feet of the chestnut, but he could not close the gap any further.

Daniel did not really hear Barton screaming, "Isobel!" above the noise of the crowd. But the name trickled through to him somehow. He glanced toward the bleachers.

Isobel had yanked loose. Barton was chasing her, a useless gesture since his waddling run was even more stilted than hers. Dragging her leash, she bucketed out onto the track and ran to join her best friend.

Now the mystery runner and Tornado were coming out of the far turn. There were too few yards left until the finish line. Tornado would never catch him now. Then Isobel was running alongside the pack, falling in beside her friend, running free and happy with Tornado as she had done so often in the wash.

Tornado was accustomed to it.

But the mystery race horse was not. Because of those fancy blinders, the chestnut was slow to notice the little javelina. Suddenly there she was, an alien presence right beside him! Wild-eyed with panic, the mystery horse squealed and bolted sideways. As the crowd gasped and moaned, the sleek racing machine lunged over the inside rail and galloped off across the infield, nose high and tail out.

Tornado was the winner at forty to one!

Pop and Daniel relaxed against the railpost. Daniel felt as weak as if he himself had run that mile. Neither of them heard the stomping crowds. Neither knew what should be said next. Finally, Pop muttered, "Well, now that you're rich, what are you going to do with your winnings?"

"What would you want me to do?"

"Cash in your ticket, keep five and refuse the rest."

Daniel stared at Pop.

Pop continued. "Principles are principles. You don't go bending them because it's convenient to. Or even because it's profitable."

Daniel grinned. "I'm sure glad you said that! I couldn't do it!" He fished in his pocket and dragged out the five dollars in all its many pieces. "You see, Pop, Matt and I were talking yesterday, and I've given my life to Jesus, even if I don't know exactly what it all means yet. Two hundred dollars we would've won, and that's so much money. I argued with myself a lot. But I knew all along that you and Mom and Jesus didn't want me betting. So I ended up not doing it."

Daniel handed the money to Pop. His pockets were deeper than Daniel's. Daniel felt awfully good. "You know, Pop, we won!"

Pop was grinning so broadly his face was two pieces. "We sure did, Dan. We all won. Let's go see Chet."

The megaphone voice was barking again.

"Wait. Listen," said Pop. "The outsider called a foul."

"A what?"

"He complained to the track stewards. That means that Tornado may not have won after all. Let's go!"

There was a big crowd around Chet, his horse, and his pig. Pop and Daniel jostled their way through. When one burly cowboy turned to glare at them, Daniel shrugged. "The pig's an old friend of mine," he said and pushed on past.

Chet was throwing a blanket over Tornado. Daniel helped him straighten it on the other side.

"What's happening?" Daniel asked.

"That stranger filed a protest because the pig ran out on the track. We might get disqualified after all. Pa's over with the track stewards now."

Chet's pa appeared from the ring of spectators and joined them. "H'lo, Tremain. Dan'l."

Daniel nodded.

Pop said, "Clay."

"Well?" asked Chet.

"Don't know yet. The stewards heard both sides, and now they're deliberating." He turned to Pop. "Ira, this here afternoon has made me an old man. Everything we have is riding on this race."

"Hope there's a lesson here for you, Clay, win or lose."

"You bet there is! Never again am I gonna bet a single penny on anything. Not anything. Say—uh—how much did you put on Tornado?"

"Didn't bet."

"Not even a teeny bit?"

"Not a betting man, Clay."

Chet's pa studied Pop closely. He cleared his throat.

"You put your money where your mouth is, don't you, Ira."

Daniel nodded. "Principles are principles. You can't go bending 'm just because it's convenient or profitable."

Chet hissed. "Here's the steward!"

The crowd quieted—at least the people nearby did. The steward, a short dumpy gentleman, cleared his throat and proclaimed loudly, "The stewards have considered the protest of Mr. Harold McElvy. Because the musk hog got out on the track accidentally and without malicious intent, and because all the entrants saw said musk hog but only the one horse bolted, the stewards declare this a fair race. The standings remain as posted."

Chet whooped and grabbed Daniel. They laughed and hooted and waltzed each other in a happy circle. "We won! We won! We won!"

Daniel was laughing so hard his eyes were crying. "All the local horses know javelina when they smell it. They wouldn't shy!"

Chet was laughing just as hard. "That's right! It's only the city-bred horse who got worried!"

Chet's pa was pumping Pop's hand. "That pig's the best investment I ever made, Ira. It just saved my farm!"

Barton came running up, a sheaf of bills in his hand. "I just cashed in the tickets, Pa! Looka here! Jes' lookit!"

Chet's pa snatched the money from Barton's hand without counting it. He divided out a part of the wad and thrust it into Pop's hand. "Here!"

Pop pulled back. "I couldn't take that, Clay."

"Yes, you will!" Chet's pa's face was almost grim. "Hit's a free gift. I don't give gifts easy, Ira. Ain't my nature. It's a gift because I—uh—I admire you. How you stand up for what you know is right."

Pop started to protest, but Daniel cut him off. "Take it, Pop!"

"What?"

"Take it. I just remember. Matt was telling me about free gifts when we were walking back from the millpond. He said a free gift is the hardest thing in the world to accept. You always feel like you have to earn it somehow. But God's love is free. So is His forgiveness, just like that money. It's the easiest thing and the hardest thing all at once. And another thing," Daniel cut his father's protest short again, "I told Matt about the bad winter ahead, and he said just pray to God to provide. He will. Well, He just did."

Chet's pa smirked, "Dan'l, you ain't calling me a long arm of God, are ya?"

Daniel shrugged. "Sure. Why not? He loves you just as much as anyone else. Why shouldn't He use you?"

"I ain't a—uh—a religious man."

"Well, yesterday I was religious, but I still didn't belong to God. There's a difference."

Pop was all tied up in emotional knots of some sort. He sure was thinking fast. "Nope. Principles are principles. I thank you, Clay. Much as I'd like to, I can't take it. But I appreciate you offering it. Your generosity means a lot to me. Like Dan says, The Lord will provide for us. Now we're all going out to dinner at the hotel. Your boys, mine, us. And then you and I are going over to Carsons' to talk to Matt. We need what he's got. Both of us do. That boy has answers to questions I'm too dumb to even ask. And my wife's been some troubled. Bet he can solve Martha's questions, too, I think."

Chet's pa stammered around at something, but Pop clapped a lanky arm across his shoulder. "Come on, Clay! This is the only time in my whole life I'll ever get to take a winning racehorse owner out to dinner. Coming, Chet?"

Chet grinned. "You bet! Barton'll join us just as soon as he's through. Bart, after you cool out Tornado and pen up Isobel, fetch on over to the hotel."

Barton was so angry his red face glowed livid.

Daniel tapped Pop's arm. "I'll join you there in a little while, Pop. Come on, Barton, I'll help. It won't take long."

He grabbed Isobel's leash, and Barton led Tornado away. The little javelina actually seemed glad to see Daniel again. As he stooped down to scratch her she stuffed her wiggly snout into his shirt and nuzzled him. She rooted out his shirttail, grunting.

Isobel, a beautiful thing, devoted to God.

Daniel rubbed her neck and shoulders, laughing. "Isobel, you beautiful musk hog, you . . ."

Moody Press, a ministry of the Moody Bible Institute, is designed for education, evangelization, and edification. If we may assist you in knowing more about Christ and the Christian life, please write us without obligation: Moody Press, c/o MLM, Chicago, Illinois 60610.